THE HOUND OF THE BASKERVILLES

The *Oxford Progressive English Reader*s series provides a wide range of reading for learners of English.

Each book in the series has been written to follow the strict guidelines of a syllabus, wordlist and structure list. The texts are graded according to these guidelines; Grade 1 at a 1,400 word level, Grade 2 at a 2,100 word level, Grade 3 at a 3,100 word level, Grade 4 at a 3,700 word level and Grade 5 at a 5,000 word level.

The latest methods of text analysis, using specially designed software, ensure that readability is carefully controlled at every level. Any new words which are vital to the mood and style of the story are explained within the text, and reoccur throughout for maximum reinforcement. New language items are also clarified by attractive illustrations.

Each book has a short section containing carefully graded exercises and controlled activities, which test both global and specific understanding.

The Hound of the Baskervilles

Sir Arthur Conan Doyle

1992
Hong Kong
Oxford University Press
Oxford Singapore Tokyo

Oxford University Press

Oxford   New York   Toronto
Kuala Lumpur   Singapore   Hong Kong   Tokyo
Delhi   Bombay   Calcutta   Madras   Karachi
Nairobi   Dar es Salaam   Cape Town
Melbourne   Auckland

and associated companies in
Berlin   Ibadan

Illustrated by Jon Berkeley

Syllabus designer: David Foulds

Text processing and analysis by Luxfield Consultants Ltd.

ISBN 0 19 585432 2

Printed in Hong Kong
Published by Oxford University Press,
18/F Warwick House, Tong Chong Street,
Quarry Bay, Hong Kong

CONTENTS

CONTENTS

MR SHERLOCK HOLMES

The walking stick

Mr Sherlock Holmes sat near the breakfast table. I was standing by the window. We were both thinking about a visitor who had come while we were out. We had not seen him, but he had left his walking stick behind, ⁵ and, at that moment, I was holding it in my hands, looking at it carefully.

It was a fine piece of wood. There was a broad band of silver at the top, on which was written: 'To James Mortimer, M.R.C.S. from his friends of the C.C.H., 1884.' ¹⁰

'What do you think?' said Holmes. 'We did not see him, and we do not know why he wanted to see us, so this stick is very important.'

'Well, "M.R.C.S." tells us that he is a doctor. And I think he must be an old man because he uses a walking ¹⁵ stick. I also think that he is quite rich and that he has a number of friends.' I had learnt some of Holmes's methods, but I could never be as clever as he was.

'Good,' said Holmes.

'Dr Mortimer seems to be a doctor in a village,' I ²⁰ continued. 'He often walks to the houses of his patients.'

'Why do you think so?'

'This stick was very beautiful at one time. But it has been used a lot and it is not so good now. No doctor in a town would carry a stick that looks like this.'

'Very good,' said Holmes. ²⁵

'I think the letters "C.C.H." mean some sort of club, perhaps a hunting club. Dr Mortimer must have helped them. That is why they gave him this stick.'

'You have done very well, Watson,' said Holmes.

Holmes had never said this before. I felt very pleased and proud.

Sherlock Holmes took the stick from me and looked
5   at it carefully.

'Did I forget anything?' I asked.

'I am afraid, my dear Watson, that you have made a few mistakes. You are not all wrong though. The man is a doctor in a village, and he walks a lot.'

10   'Then I was right.'

'Only on these points.'

'But what else can you learn from the stick?'

'We can learn much more, Watson, much more. A hunting club does not usually give a present of this kind
15   to a doctor. A hospital often does. The letter "H" in "C.C.H." could stand for "hospital". There cannot be many hospitals that have two names beginning with the letter "C". "C.C. Hospital" probably means Charing Cross Hospital.'

20   'You may be right.'

'It is most likely.'

'Well, let us say C.C.H. does stand for Charing Cross Hospital. If that is true it only means that
25   the man was a town doctor before he became a country doctor.'

'We can say more than that. Let us ask ourselves why he
30   was given this present. We think that Dr Mortimer left the hospital to work in the country, so his friends could have given him the walking stick when he left.'

35   'That seems possible.'

'Now there is one other point. Dr Mortimer could not have been working at Charing Cross Hospital. Only a good London doctor would be working there, and a good London doctor would not leave and go to work in a village. What was Dr Mortimer doing then? He was in the hospital, yet he was not working there. Therefore, he must have been a student doctor at Charing Cross Hospital. And we know, from the date on the stick, that he left five years ago. You were wrong when you said that he is an old man, Watson. If Dr Mortimer was a student only five years ago then he must be a young man under thirty years old.'

'Well, that does seem to be possible.'

'So, my dear Watson,' continued Holmes, getting up and taking the walking stick from my hands, 'we now know that the owner of this stick is a young man, a friendly sort of person, and not very ambitious — if he wanted to be a famous doctor he would not have gone to work in a village. He is also rather forgetful.'

He moved to the window in order to see the stick more clearly. 'Oh, yes,' he added, 'and he has a favourite dog, which is larger than a terrier, but smaller than a mastiff.'

'A dog?'

'Yes, a dog that often walks behind his master, carrying the stick in his mouth. This stick is quite heavy, so the dog has to hold it tightly by the middle. Look, you can see the marks made by his teeth very easily. The distance between the two sets of marks tells me the size of the dog's mouth, and that, of course, tells me the size of the dog. As you can see, Watson, a medium-sized dog would have made these marks.'

Holmes paused, and looked very thoughtful. Then he continued, 'In fact I am sure, now, that it is a golden-brown curly-haired spaniel.'

'But Holmes, how can you possibly know ... '

'Because,' answered Holmes, looking through the window into the street, 'the dog, and his master, have just come to the front door.'

5   At that moment the door-bell rang, and a few seconds later Mrs Hudson, Holmes's housekeeper, showed someone into the room.

I was very surprised to see our visitor. He did not look like a country doctor at all. He was a tall, thin, man, about thirty years old. He had a long nose and he wore glasses. As soon as he came in, he saw the walking stick in Holmes's hands.

'Oh, I am so glad,' he said. 'I did not know whether I had left it here or somewhere else. I would be very sad if I lost that stick.'

25   'A present from Charing Cross Hospital?' asked Holmes.

'Yes, sir.'

'Then I was right,' said Holmes, looking quite pleased with himself.

The legend

30   Holmes invited our visitor to sit down. As he did so, he took some papers from his pocket. They were yellow with age.

'I have brought this letter with me,' said Dr Mortimer, handing the papers to Holmes. 'It was written in 1742.

35   My friend, Sir Charles Baskerville asked me to keep it

for him. Sir Charles died three months ago, and he knew that he was going to die before it happened. Now, neither of us believed in ghosts, Mr Holmes, but Sir Charles believed what this letter said. It warned him about something, you see.'

Holmes took the letter, and began to examine it.

'It seems to be a report,' said Holmes.

'Yes, it is about a legend which concerns the Baskerville family. With your permission, I will read it to you.'

Holmes sat back in his chair and closed his eyes. Dr Mortimer began to read.

'"About a hundred years ago, Baskerville Hall was owned by a relative with the same name as mine, Hugo Baskerville. He was a wild and cruel man. Hugo loved the daughter of a farmer, but she did not like him and was afraid of his cruel ways.

'"One day Hugo went to the girl's farm with five or six of his evil friends. They carried the girl away, brought her to Baskerville Hall and locked her in a room upstairs.

'"The girl was very frightened, but she managed to escape through a window. Then she started running towards her home which was nine miles away, across the moor.

'"A little later, Hugo came to the room with some food, and found it empty. He became very angry. He called to his friends to help him catch the girl. They were surprised at his anger. One of them joked that Hugo should let the hunting dogs chase after the girl. When he heard this, Hugo immediately ran out of the house. He shouted to his servants to get his horse ready, and to let the hounds out.

'"His friends suddenly realized that Hugo was going to do something terrible. They ran out to stop him, but it was too late; Hugo and the hounds had already gone. Hugo's friends got on their horses and chased across the moor, after him.

‘"When they had gone a few miles they met a
5 shepherd. They asked him if he had seen Hugo and the hounds. The shepherd was very frightened. He could hardly speak. He said that he had seen the girl, then the hounds chasing the girl, then Hugo following the hounds, and then, running after Hugo, another
10 animal that looked like a hound but was much bigger.

‘"The men became frightened when they heard this. They rode very close to one another. Soon afterwards they met Hugo's hounds running back towards them with their tails between their legs, and crying in fear.

15 ‘"A mile further on, they stopped. In front of them they could see the girl lying on the ground, dead. The body of Hugo Baskerville lay beside her. And standing over Hugo was a very big animal. It was like a hound, but as large as a small horse. This terrible creature
20 suddenly turned its face towards them, and the men screamed out loudly and quickly rode away.

‘"This is the legend of the Hound of the Baskervilles. It has caused a lot of trouble for the family since that day.
25 A number of family members have died strangely and suddenly. Nobody knows why.

‘"I therefore advise you not to go out on the
30 moor when it is dark."

‘(This letter was written by Hugo Baskerville to his sons Rodger
35 and John).’

THE PROBLEM

The death of Sir Charles Baskerville

When Dr Mortimer finished reading the letter, he took something out of his pocket. It was a folded newspaper.

'Now, Mr Holmes. This is the *Devonshire County Chronicle* of the 14th of June this year.'

Our visitor began to read from the newspaper.

'"The death of Sir Charles Baskerville has come as a great shock to many people, and it is still not clear how he died. Some say that he did not die from natural causes, but this cannot be true. Nobody killed him. Sir Charles died of a heart attack.

'"Sir Charles lived very simply at Baskerville Hall. His butler, Barrymore, and Barrymore's wife, the housekeeper, have both said that Sir Charles was in poor health. Dr James Mortimer, Sir Charles's doctor and friend, agrees.

'"Every night, before going to bed, Sir Charles Baskerville took a walk in the Yew Alley next to his house. In the evening of the 4th of June, after saying that he wanted to go to London the next day and asking Barrymore to pack his luggage for him, Sir Charles went out for his walk in the Alley as usual. Sadly, he never came back.

'"At twelve o'clock, Barrymore found the hall door still open. He took a lamp and went out to look for Sir Charles.

'"It had been raining earlier, so Sir Charles's foot-marks could easily be seen. Half-way down the alley,

there is a gate which leads to the moor. The footprints showed that Sir Charles had stood at that gate for some time. They changed further along the alley, where he seems to have been walking on his toes. Then, at the end of the alley, Barrymore found Sir Charles's body.

'"There was nothing to show that Sir Charles had been attacked. But there was a terrible look on his face. However, this often happens when a person dies of heart failure, and we know that Sir Charles did have a very weak heart.

'"Sir Charles's heir is his nephew, Sir Henry Baskerville, who has been living in Canada and America for some years."

'This,' said Dr Mortimer, 'is what most people know about Sir Charles Baskerville's death, Mr Holmes.'

'Thank you,' said Sherlock Holmes. 'Are you saying that there are other facts that have not appeared in the newspaper?'

'Yes.'

'Then please tell me.'

'Very few people live on the moor. Those who live there know each other well. That was why I often saw Sir Charles. He lived very quietly and was a sick man. We also had the same hobby. We were both interested in science. The only other educated people on the moor are Mr Frankland of Lafter Hall, Mr Stapleton, who studies plants and animals, and his sister, who is a very pretty woman.

'During the last few months, I could see that Sir Charles had become a very frightened man. He believed in this legend, and he really thought something evil could happen to his family. He knew that many of his relatives had died in terrible ways. He kept thinking that something was following him. He often asked me whether I had seen a strange animal on the moor close to Baskerville Hall, or if I had heard the cries of a large hound.

'One evening I drove to his house. This was three weeks before he died. Sir Charles was at the hall door. I got down from my carriage and stood in front of him. But he did not look at me. He was staring at the moor. There was a very frightened look on his face.

'I turned around. In the distance I saw an animal running across the hillside. It was black, and about the size of a small horse. Sir Charles became excited. He was very frightened.

'I stayed with him all that evening. He told me about his great fear. That was when he showed me the letter and asked me to keep it.

'I knew Sir Charles had a weak heart. I advised him to go to London where he would feel safer. I thought a bad fright would kill him. But before anything could be done, he died.

'It was Barrymore who discovered Sir Charles's body. He sent someone to fetch me. I was still awake at that time. I reached Baskerville Hall about an hour later.

'I studied the place where Sir Charles's body was found very carefully. I followed the footprints down the Yew Alley. I noticed that Sir Charles had stood at the gate. I saw the change in his footprints after the gate.

I also saw the footprints that had been made by
Barrymore as he searched for Sir Charles.

'I carefully examined the body. Nobody had touched
it until my arrival. Sir Charles lay on his face. His arms
were spread out and his fingers were dug into the
ground. There was a very frightened look on his face.
But there were no signs on the body to show that he
had been hurt by anyone.

'At the inquest, Barrymore said something which was
not true. He said there were no marks on the ground
near the body. He did not see any, but I did. They were
further away from the body, and were very clear.'

'Footprints?' asked Holmes.

'Yes, footprints.'

'A man's or a woman's?'

Dr Mortimer looked strangely at us for a moment.
His voice became very soft as he answered.

'Mr Holmes, they were the
footprints of a very large
dog.'

The good detective

I was shocked when I heard these words. Holmes, however, was very excited. He had become greatly interested in the story. 'You saw this?'

'Yes, I saw it very clearly.'   5

'And you said nothing?'

'What was the use?'

'Why didn't anybody else see the footprints?'

'They were about twenty yards from the body. If I had not known about the legend, I would not have   10 thought to look.'

'Are there many sheep-dogs on the moor?'

'Yes, but this was not a sheep-dog.'

'You say it was large?'

'It was very large.'   15

'But it did not come near the body?'

'No.'

'What is the alley like?'

'There are two lines of hedge. They are twelve feet high and very thick. The path between them is about   20 eight feet wide. At each side, there is a strip of grass. This is about six feet wide.'

'And there is a gate in the hedge?'

'Yes, this leads to the moor.'

'Is there any other opening?'   25

'No.'

'This means that there are only two ways of getting into Yew Alley. One is from the house, and the other is through the gate.'

'There is one other way. That is through a small   30 building — a summer-house — at the far end,' said Dr Mortimer.

'Had Sir Charles reached this?'

'No, he was about fifty yards from it.'

'Now, tell me, Dr Mortimer, was the gate closed?'

'It was closed and locked.'

'How high is it?'

'About four feet high.'

5 'Then anyone could have climbed over it?'

'Yes.'

'Did you see any marks near the gate?'

'They were not very clear. Sir Charles must have stood there for five or ten minutes.'

10 'How do you know that?'

'He had been smoking a cigar, and the ash had dropped onto the ground, twice.'

'Very good! Watson, Dr Mortimer is a good detective. But what about the footmarks?'

15 'He had left his own marks all over that piece of ground. I did not see any other marks.'

'I wish I had been there!' Holmes said. 'This is a very interesting case. I could have learnt many things from the marks on the ground. But it is too late now. They 20 will have been washed away by the rain. Oh, why didn't you call me earlier, Dr Mortimer?'

'I do not think even the best detective could have done anything.'

'You mean that you think the thing is supernatural 25 — that Sir Charles was killed by some kind of ghost?'

'I am not sure, but since Sir Charles died, Mr Holmes, I have heard of many strange things.'

'For example?'

'Before Sir Charles's death, several people had seen 30 something on the moor. These people agreed that it was a large animal, with a strange blue, ghostly light all around it. It was very frightening. I have talked to two of them. One was a man who has lived on the moor for many years, and the other was a farmer. They 35 both told me the same story. They both think the animal they saw was the Baskerville Hound. Many of the people living in the district are very frightened. Only the bravest will cross the moor at night.'

'You are a doctor. Do you really think this is something supernatural?'

'I do not know what to believe.'

'Well, you must admit, Dr Mortimer, that the footprints were real.'

'The original hound was able to kill a man. Yet, it was also supernatural.'

'I see that you believe strongly in supernatural things. But now, Dr Mortimer, tell me this. Why did you come to me? You believe this case is a supernatural case, but I am only a human detective.'

'Because I want your advice. The heir, Sir Charles's nephew, Sir Henry Baskerville, will be arriving at Waterloo Station,' — Dr Mortimer looked at his watch — 'in one hour and fifteen minutes. The problem is, I do not know what to do.'

'I think, sir, you should take a carriage, and go to Waterloo Station to meet him.'

'And then?'

'Don't tell him anything yet. Let me think about the whole matter first.'

'How long will you take?'

'Twenty-four hours. Come back to see me at ten o'clock tomorrow morning, and bring Sir Henry Baskerville with you.'

'I will do so, Mr Holmes.'

'Thank you. Good morning.'

After saying this, Holmes returned to his seat. He looked satisfied. This meant that he had something pleasant to do.

SIR HENRY BASKERVILLE

Thinking about the case

I knew that Holmes wanted to think about what he had heard, and he needed to be alone. I therefore spent the rest of the day at my club, and did not return to Baker
5   Street until later that evening.

When I walked into his smoke-filled study, Holmes had a map in his hands. He showed it to me.

'This is the district that we are interested in,' he said. 'It shows us a part of Dartmoor, in Devonshire. That is
10   Baskerville Hall in the middle. The Yew Alley is not marked here, but I think it must be along this line. The moor is to the right of it. These buildings here are the village of Grimpen. Dr Mortimer has his office here. There are very few houses for miles around. Here is
15   Lafter Hall. That house there is probably Stapleton's. Here are two farmhouses. Fourteen miles away is the prison at Princetown. The whole area is empty moorland.'

'Dartmoor must be a very wild place.'

'There are two things we have to ask ourselves. First,
20   has there been a crime? Remember, nobody actually killed Sir Charles. Second, what was the crime, and how was it committed? Dr Mortimer believes that something supernatural caused Sir Charles's death. If this is true, then there is nothing we can do. But we must find out
25   if human beings had something to do with it.'

'I have been thinking about the case all day. It is very puzzling.'

'I agree, it is very unusual. The change in the foot-prints; why should a man walk on his toes down an
30   alley?'

'Well, what do you think, Holmes?'

'I think he was running. He was running for his life. He had a weak heart, and the running killed him. So he fell dead upon his face.'

'Running from what?'

'That is what we have to find out! The man was very frightened before he ran. There is proof of this.'

'Why do you say that?'

'I believe something on the moor must have frightened him. That is why he ran. Now, if you were frightened, you would run towards the house. But Sir Charles was mad with fear. He could not think clearly. So he ran away from the house. And who was he waiting for that night? Why did he wait in the Yew Alley? Why didn't he wait inside the house?'

'You think that he was waiting for someone?'

'We know Sir Charles was old, and in poor health. The newspaper article said that he went out every evening, but I do not believe he would have gone out when the weather was cold and wet unless he had a very good reason. Dr Mortimer thinks that Sir Charles stood in the Yew Alley for five or ten minutes. He must have been waiting for someone, someone that he did not want the servants at Baskerville Hall to see. He was planning to leave for London the next morning. The night before he was going to leave, he waited to meet someone in the alley. It is beginning to make sense, Watson. But we will not think about it any more now. Let us wait until we see Dr Mortimer and Sir Henry Baskerville, tomorrow morning.'

A strange letter

Dr Mortimer came at ten o'clock the following morning with a small, dark-eyed man about thirty years old. This was the young Sir Henry Baskerville.

'I have always wanted to see you myself, Mr Holmes,' said Sir Henry. 'I hear that you are a very good detective. Now I have a puzzle for you already.'

'Please take a seat, Sir Henry. Has something strange
5   happened to you so soon?'

'I think it is a kind of a joke, Mr Holmes. It is a letter which reached me this morning.' He put a cheap grey envelope on the table. The address, 'Sir Henry Baskerville, Northumberland Hotel,' was badly written.
10   The letter had been posted the evening before, from Charing Cross.

'Who knew that you were going to stay at the Northumberland Hotel?' asked Holmes.

'No one; I only decided
15   to stay there after I met Dr Mortimer.'

'Were you staying there, Dr Mortimer, before you met
20   Sir Henry?'

'No, I have been staying with a friend,' said the doctor. 'No one could have
25   known that we were going to stay at this hotel.'

'So, the explanation is that someone must have been following you. That is the only way he could have known your address.'

30   Holmes took out the letter from the envelope. He opened it and put it on the table. There was only one sentence in the letter: *If you value your life keep away from the moor.* All the words, except one, had been cut from a newspaper, but the word 'moor' had been
35   written in ink.

'Mr Holmes, please tell me what this letter means. Who sent it to me? Why should he be so interested in me?'

'What do you think, Dr Mortimer? The letter has clearly been sent by a human being. It has not been sent by a ghost.'   5

'No,' replied Dr Mortimer, 'but it might have been sent by a person who believes there is something strange at Baskerville Hall.'

'What are you all talking about?' asked Sir Henry. 'You gentlemen seem to know more about my own   10 business than I do.'

'We'll tell you about it later, Sir Henry. I promise you,' said Sherlock Holmes. 'But, first, let us look at your letter. It was put together and posted yesterday evening. Do we still have a copy of yesterday's *Times*, Watson?'   15

'It is here in the corner.'

'Can you please bring it?'

Holmes quickly looked through the newspaper. 'Yes, there is a very good article here about Free Trade,' he said. 'Let me read this part to you.   20

"If you think that your own special trade or your industry will benefit from higher import duties, you will be wrong. There is every reason to believe that these new laws will reduce the value of our currency, keep away wealth from the country, and   25 lower the general standards of life in this island."

'What do you think of that?' cried Holmes. He looked very pleased, and rubbed his hands together.

The writer

Dr Mortimer and Sir Henry Baskerville looked at me.   30
They were both puzzled.

'I do not understand,' said Sir Henry. 'I know nothing about Free Trade, and it does not tell us anything about the letter.'

'It tells us a great deal,' said Holmes. 'The letter comes from the newspaper article. All the printed words in the letter appear in it — "If you', "your", "life", "value", "keep away", "from the".'

5   'You are right!' cried Sir Henry. 'That is very clever of you. How did you know?'

'I study the printing types used by different newspapers. By looking at the type in the letter, I knew it came from the *Times*. The letter was sent yesterday.

10   So the person who sent it probably used yesterday's *Times*.'

'But why was the word "moor" handwritten?' asked Sir Henry.

'Because he could not find

15   that word anywhere in the newspaper. The other words were all simple, and can be found in many newspapers. But the word

20   "moor" is not common.'

'So that is why it was handwritten. What else have you learnt from the letter, Mr Holmes?'

'The address is written in very bad handwriting. You might think that the person who wrote it is not well-

25   educated. But the *Times* is a newspaper read by well-educated people. Therefore, I think the letter was sent by a well-educated person. He wrote the address roughly on purpose. He wanted you to think that he is an uneducated person. He has not written the letter in

30   his usual handwriting. This tells us that he is afraid you might recognize it. Therefore, I also think he is a person whom you know, or will soon know.' Then he turned to Sir Henry, saying, 'And now, Sir Henry, has anything else unusual happened to you since you arrived in

35   London?'

ONE MISSING BOOT

Sir Henry is surprised

Sir Henry looked uncertain for a second or two. Then he smiled.

'I have lost one of my boots. I have lived most of my life in Canada and the United States, so I do not know if this is usual or not here? Do people often lose their boots in London?'

'You have lost just one of your boots?'

'Well, I do not know where it is now. I put both boots outside my door last night, to be polished. In the morning, there was only one left. No one at the hotel could tell me anything. I only bought those boots yesterday. I had not even put them on.'

'You bought them yesterday?'

'Yes, I bought some clothes yesterday. Dr Mortimer went to the shops with me. Those boots cost me six dollars. And one has been stolen before I have even worn them!'

'One boot is a useless thing to steal,' said Sherlock Holmes. 'But I think it will soon be found.'

'I certainly hope so,' said Sir Henry. He continued, 'Now, gentlemen, I have told you everything I know. It is time you kept your promise to tell me all that you know.'

Dr Mortimer then took out his letter and the copy of the *Devonshire County Chronicle*, and told his story. Sir Henry Baskerville listened with great attention. He was very surprised.

When Dr Mortimer finished, Sir Henry said, 'I have heard about the hound ever since I was a child, but I never really believed in it. You don't seem to be sure about my uncle's death. Did somebody kill him, or did he die of a heart attack?'

'That is what we don't know, Sir Henry. We have to decide now whether or not you should go to Baskerville Hall.'

'But why should I not go?'

'There seems to be some danger.'

'What sort of danger? From this hound, or from human beings?'

'Well, that is what we have to discover.'

'Whatever it is, I shall go. I am not worried about any ghost or any human being. Baskerville Hall is the home of my family, and that is where I am going to live. I will not change my mind. But I must think about what you have told me and I would like to be alone for an hour. It's half past eleven, now, Mr Holmes. I am going straight back to my hotel. Would you and Dr Watson come and see Dr Mortimer and me at two? We will have lunch together. Then I'll tell you what I think about the whole business.'

At the Northumberland Hotel

Sherlock Holmes and I reached the Northumberland Hotel just before two o'clock that afternoon.

'Sir Henry Baskerville is waiting for you upstairs,' said the clerk. 'He asked me to show you to his room.'

We followed the clerk. At the top of the stairs, we met Sir Henry. He was very angry. He was holding a boot in one hand. It was black, and looked rather worn.

'The people in this hotel think I am a fool,' he cried. 'They had better be careful. If that man can't find my missing boot, I am going to be very angry.'

'Still looking for your boot?' asked Holmes.

'Yes, and I want to find it!'

'But you said your boots were brown and new.'

'That's right. Now I have lost one of my old black boots.'

'Are you saying someone has stolen another one?'

'Yes, that's exactly what I am saying. Last night, they took my brown boot. Today they have stolen the black one!'

Sir Henry turned angrily to a German waiter who had just come in. 'Well, have you found it yet?' he shouted. The man was very frightened.

'No, sir. Nobody has seen your boot.'

'You had better find it soon. Otherwise, I'll see the manager and leave this hotel.'

'It shall be found, sir, I promise you. Please be patient.'

'You make sure that you do find it. I am not going to lose any more things in this hotel. It's full of thieves.' Then, turning to us, he said, 'Oh, please forgive me for all this trouble, Mr Holmes.'

'I think it's trouble we should know about.'

'It's very strange, don't you think?'

'Well, I do not understand it yet. This case is very difficult, Sir Henry. But we now have several facts to think about. One of them will lead us to the truth.'

We then had a pleasant lunch, during which we said very little about the case.

The money and the property

After lunch, we went to Sir Henry's private sitting-room.
Holmes asked him what he planned to do.

'I shall go to Baskerville Hall at the end of the week.'

5   'I think that would be the right thing to do,' said
Holmes. 'It seems that somebody is following you
around, but London is so crowded, it is difficult to find
out who it is. We do not know what he wants. He might
want to harm you, and we would not be able to protect

10   you in London.'

'I must say one thing,' said Baskerville. 'If none of
the Baskervilles live in the Hall because of that hound,
the servants, Barrymore and his wife, will have little
work. They will also have a very nice house to live in.'

15   'When Sir Charles died, did Barrymore get anything,
Dr Mortimer?' asked Holmes.

'Under Sir Charles's will, he and his wife got five
hundred pounds each.'

'Ha! Did they know that they would get the money

20   if Sir Charles died?'

'Yes, Sir Charles liked to talk about his will.'

'That is very interesting.'

'I hope,' said Dr Mortimer, 'that you do not suspect
everyone who received money from Sir Charles when

25   he died. I too received a thousand pounds.'

'Indeed! And anyone else?'

'There were small amounts of money given to a
number of people. Most of it, however, almost seven
hundred and fifty thousand pounds, goes to Sir Henry.'

30   Holmes looked surprised.

'Dear me! That is a lot of money. A criminal would
do almost anything to get his hands on that much. One
more question, Dr Mortimer. If something happens to
Sir Henry, who would get the property?'

'Sir Charles had a younger brother, Rodger Baskerville, but he died unmarried. So the property would go to the Desmonds. They are cousins of the Baskervilles. James Desmond lives in Westmorland. He is quite an old man.'

'Have you met Mr James Desmond?'

'Yes, he came to visit Sir Charles once. He looked very respectable. Sir Charles wanted to give him a sum of money, but Desmond did not want to take it.'

'And this man would be the heir to Sir Charles's fortune?'

'He would get Baskerville Hall, but not the money. Sir Henry can do what he likes with that. But if Sir Henry does not make a will of his own, then the money will also go to Desmond.'

'And have you made your will, Sir Henry?'

'No, Mr Holmes, I have not. I've had no time. I only knew about the whole thing yesterday. But I feel that the money should go with the property. My uncle wanted it this way. Baskerville Hall is a large house, and the owner must have money to look after it. Therefore, I feel that the house, land and money must all go together.'

'Well, Sir Henry, I agree with you that you must go to Dartmoor immediately, but you must not go alone.'

'Dr Mortimer is coming back with me.'

'But Dr Mortimer has his work to do. And his house is many miles away from yours. Dr Mortimer may want to help you very much, but he cannot be with you all the time. No, Sir Henry, you must take someone with you — a person whom you can trust, and who will always be near you.'

'Would you be able to come yourself, Mr Holmes?'

'I will be there later, but I have a lot of work to do in London. I cannot go away for some time.'

'Who do you think should go with me?'

Dr Watson agrees

Holmes put his hand on my arm.

'I hope Dr Watson here will agree to go. He is the best man. He would be able to help you if you were in trouble.'

5   I was very surprised, but before I could say anything, Sir Henry shook my hand.

'Well, now, that is very kind of you, Dr Watson,' he said. 'You know about the whole matter. I'll be very happy if you come to Baskerville Hall with me.'

10   'I will be very happy to come with you,' I replied.

'And you will report to me everything that you find out, Watson,' said Holmes. 'Something is going to happen, I am quite sure. I will tell you what to do when the time comes. Would you be ready to go by Saturday,

15   Sir Henry?'

'Would Dr Watson be ready by then?'

'Yes,' I replied.

'Then we will all meet at Paddington Station on Saturday morning. The train leaves at 10.30.'

20   Baskerville suddenly gave a cry of excitement. He hurried across the room to a small cupboard, and from beneath it pulled out a shiny, new brown boot.

'My missing boot!' he cried.

5

BASKERVILLE HALL

Baskerville Hall

On Saturday morning, Holmes went with me to the railway station. On the way there he told me what he wanted me to do.

'I will not say what I think about this case yet,' he said. 'All I want you to do is to report to me when you are at Baskerville Hall. Let me know about anything which you think is connected with the case. Find out as much as you can about Sir Charles's death. Study the people living near Baskerville Hall. Watch them all very carefully, even those you think you can trust. One of them might be guilty.'

'I will do my best.'

'You have a small gun with you, I suppose?'

'Yes, I thought I might need it.'

Our friends were already waiting for us at the railway station.

'We have not heard anything new,' said Dr Mortimer. 'But I am very sure of one thing. Nobody followed us during the last two days. Every time we went out, we kept a careful watch. We did not see anyone.'

'If you stayed together I do not believe anyone would trouble you. Sir Henry, you must never go out alone. I feel sure that something will happen to you if you do. Did you get back your other boot?'

'No, I think I have lost it for ever.'

'Indeed, that is very interesting. Well, goodbye,' said Holmes as the train began to move. 'Sir Henry, don't forget what the letter about the Baskerville legend said. Do not go out on the moor at night.'

The journey was a pleasant one. When we reached Devonshire, Sir Henry Baskerville spent some time looking out of the window. He talked about the scenery.

5   'I have been to many places in the world, Dr Watson,' he said. 'But I have never seen a place that makes me feel as happy as this does.'

'A Devonshire man always loves his home,' I said. 'You were very young when you left Baskerville Hall,
10   weren't you?'

'I was a boy when my father died. I have never seen Baskerville Hall. We lived in a different part of the country. After my father's death, I went straight to America to live with friends. I have never been here
15   before. I am very eager to see Dartmoor.'

Dr Mortimer pointed out of the window towards a line of hills. 'Well, there is the beginning of the moor now.'

Baskerville looked at the moor as the train went
20   along. He sat quietly for a long time. I knew that he was happy to be returning to his family home.

The train stopped at a small station and we got out. A carriage was waiting for us.

An escaped prisoner

25   It was a quiet peaceful place. I was surprised to see two soldiers at the station. They had guns, and looked very carefully at us. In a few minutes, we were travelling in the carriage along a broad white road. Baskerville was very happy and excited. He was
30   looking at the countryside and asking questions. Along the road, we saw a soldier on a horse. He was also carrying a gun.

'What has happened?' Dr Mortimer asked the driver. 'Why are there soldiers?'

'A criminal has escaped from the prison at Princetown, sir,' replied the driver. 'He's been out for three days now. They are watching every road and station. Nobody has seen him yet. The farmers here don't like it, sir. They are afraid. The prisoner is a very dangerous man.'

'Who is he?'

'Selden, the Notting Hill murderer.'

I remembered the name. The murderer was a very cruel person, but he was thought to be mad. That was why he had not been hanged. Instead, he had been put in prison.

We had left the green countryside and were now driving through wild moorland. Soon the driver pointed with his whip and cried out: 'Baskerville Hall!'

The house looked dark, cold and unfriendly.

'I am not surprised that my uncle became afraid, living here,' said Sir Henry. 'It's a frightening place. I'll put a row of lights in front. It won't look so bad then.'

'Welcome, Sir Henry! Welcome to Baskerville Hall!'

A tall man had come out. We could see a woman standing behind him. Both of them took our bags down from the carriage and carried them into the house.

'I must go straight home, Sir Henry,' said Dr Mortimer.

'Surely you will stay to have dinner?'

'No, I have some work to do. I would like to show you round the house, but Barrymore knows it much better than I do. Goodbye. Call me when you need me.'

The carriage drove away with the doctor in it. Sir Henry and I went inside.

'My family has lived here for five hundred years! Just think of that,' said Baskerville. 'It makes me feel rather sad.'

Barrymore came into the hall. He had taken our luggage to our rooms. He was a tall good-looking man, with a square black beard.

'Do you wish to have dinner now, sir?'

'Is it ready?'

'It will be in a few minutes, sir. And now, sir, perhaps, I can show you to your rooms.'

Our rooms were upstairs. Mine was just next to Sir Henry's. They were more modern than the other parts of the house. Both were brightly lit with candles, so they did not look so sad and frightening.

The dining-room was a dark place, full of shadows. Baskerville and I talked little as we ate our dinner. After the meal we went to another room to smoke.

'This is not a very cheerful place,' said Sir Henry. 'I'll get used to it soon, but right now, I feel very uncomfortable here. We'll go to bed early tonight. Perhaps everything will look a lot brighter in the morning.'

Before I went to sleep, I looked out of my bedroom window. In the distance, I could see the dark moor. It looked wild and empty. Suddenly the half moon broke through some clouds and covered the land with a ghostly, silver light. It made me feel afraid.

I was very tired, but I was not able to sleep. Then I heard a strange sound, like a woman crying.

I sat up in bed, immediately. The noise was not very far away. It was certainly inside the house.

I sat still, listening, for about half an hour after that. I did not hear the sound again. All I heard was the clock striking and the leaves blowing in the wind outside.   5

Stapleton introduces himself

When Sir Henry and I sat down to breakfast, it was a fine sunny morning. The sunlight came into the house through the windows. The place did not look so frightening any more.   10

'I suppose it is our fault. There is nothing wrong with the house,' said Sir Henry. 'Last night we had had a long journey. We were also feeling cold. That's why we were a bit frightened. Now we are fresh and well, and everything looks cheerful.'   15

Sir Henry had some work to do after breakfast, so I decided to take a walk to the village of Grimpen, about four miles away.

On my way back to Baskerville Hall I heard someone running behind me. A voice called out my name. I   20
turned around, thinking it would be Dr Mortimer. To my surprise, it was a stranger. He was a small man, between thirty to forty years of age. He was carrying a butterfly net.

'Please forgive me for being rude, Dr Watson,' said   25
the man. 'Down here on the moor, we are very simple people. We do not wait to be introduced to others before we talk to them. I am Stapleton, of Merripit House. I was visiting Dr Mortimer just now. You passed by the window of his office and he told me who you   30
were. Now, tell me, how is Sir Henry feeling after the journey?'

'He is very well, thank you.'

'After Sir Charles died, we were afraid that Sir Henry

might not want to live here. Does he believe in ghosts?'

'I do not think so.'

'You know the legend of the hound which is frightening the family?'

5   'I have heard it.'

'The people here will believe anything. Many of them say they have seen the creature on the moor.' Stapleton said this with a smile. 'Sir Charles believed the legend very much,' he continued. 'That was why he died. What

10   does Mr Sherlock Holmes think?'

I was surprised. How did he know about Holmes?

'Oh, I know who you are, Dr Watson,' he said. 'Everyone knows about Dr Watson, the friend of the famous detective. Something very strange has happened

15   at Baskerville Hall, and now a Dr Watson has come from London with Sir Henry. So, if you are here, it must mean that Mr Sherlock Holmes is interested in this case. What does he think, Dr Watson?'

'I am afraid I do not know, Mr Stapleton.'

20   'Will he be coming here?'

'He cannot leave London at the moment. He has other work to do.'

'What a pity! He would be able to tell us something about this case. What about your own work here? Is

25   there any way I can help you?'

'I just came to visit Sir Henry. I do not need any help.'

'Of course, of course, I do understand!' said Stapleton. 'You have to be careful. You do not want people to know what you are doing. I should not have asked anything.

30   I am sorry. I will not talk about the subject again.'

We had reached the place where there was a narrow grassy path leading from the road.

'This path leads to Merripit House. It's only a short distance from here,' said Stapleton. 'Why don't you

35   come with me? I will introduce you to my sister.'

MISS BERYL STAPLETON

A strange sound

Holmes had told me to study Sir Henry's neighbours on the moor, so when Stapleton invited me to his home I decided to go with him.

'The moor is a wonderful place,' said Stapleton, as we walked along the path to Merripit House. 'I never feel tired of it. It has many wonderful secrets.'

'Do you know it well?'

'I have only been here for two years, but I have been all over the moor. Few people here know it as well as I do.'

'Is it so hard to know?'

'Very hard. For example, do you see that great plain to the north there? That is called Grimpen Mire. You must be very careful when you go there. If you are not, you might step into a bog-hole. I saw a horse fall into one yesterday. It could not get out, and was sucked under the mud. The place is always dangerous, and after these autumn rains, it is very dangerous indeed. But I know the whole place very well. I can find my way right to the middle of it. It's a bad place, the Grimpen Mire.'

'But why do you want to go there?'

'Well, do you see those hills? They are like islands in the middle of the Mire. Many rare plants and butterflies can be found in those hills. That is why I go there.'

5   While he was speaking a very low sound came from across the moor. At first, it was very soft. Then it became a loud roar. Then it died down softly. I could not tell where the sound came from.

'What was that sound?' I cried.

10   'The farmers here say it is the Hound of the Baskervilles. I have heard it once or twice before, but never so loud.'

I looked around at the moor. I was rather afraid.

'You are an educated man. Do you believe in all that
15 nonsense?' I said. 'What do you think made that sound?'

'You hear strange noises in the Mire sometimes. It's the mud going down, or the water rising, or something.'

'No, no, that was a voice.'

'Well, perhaps it was. Have you ever heard a bittern?'
20 'No, I never have.'

'It's a rare bird. There are very few left in England. That sound may have been made by a bittern.'

'Well, it's one of the strangest sounds I have ever heard.'

'Yes, this is a very strange place. Oh, excuse me for
25 a while! That is surely …'

A small butterfly had flown near us. Stapleton quickly ran after it. The creature flew straight for the Mire. I became worried for Stapleton. He might fall into a bog-hole. But he did not stop.

30   He was still chasing it when I heard someone behind me. I looked round. A woman was coming towards me.

I was sure this must be Miss Stapleton. There were few ladies living on the moor, and someone had told me that Miss Stapleton was a beautiful woman. This
35 woman was very beautiful indeed.

The warning

She did not look like her brother at all. Stapleton had
light hair and grey eyes. Miss Stapleton's hair was very
dark, and she had beautiful black eyes. She was
graceful and tall, and had a proud face.   5

'Go back!' she said. 'Go back to London,
immediately.'

I was very surprised.

'Why should I go back?'

'I cannot explain,' she spoke quickly in a low voice.   10
'Do what I say. Never return to the moor again.'

'But I have only just arrived!'

'Man, man!' she cried. 'I am warning you for your
own good. Go back to London! Go tonight! Get away
from this place! Hush, my brother is coming! Don't tell   15
him what I said.'

Stapleton had given up his chase,
and was walking back to us.

'Hello, Beryl!' he said.

'Well, Jack, you look
very hot.'

'Yes, I was chasing a
butterfly. It is a very
rare kind, and is seldom
found in the late autumn.
I could not catch it.
What a pity!'

As he spoke, he kept
looking at the girl and at me.

'You two have introduced
yourselves, I see.'

'Yes, I was telling Sir Henry
that he has come too late, this
year, to see moor at its best.'

'Who do you think this is, then?'

'I imagine he must be Sir Henry Baskerville.'

'No, no,' said I. 'I am not Sir Henry. I am his friend, Dr Watson.'

5 Miss Stapleton's face went very red, and she said nothing.

We walked a short distance before we came to the house. It was a sad-looking place. An old manservant opened the door for us. Inside the house, the rooms 10 were large and pleasant. I looked at the moor through the windows. I wondered why the Stapletons lived here.

'Strange place to live, isn't it?' he said. He seemed to know what I was thinking. 'But we are quite happy here, aren't we, Beryl?'

15 'Quite happy,' she said. But she did not look at all happy.

'We used to live in the north of England. We had a school there but we decided to close it, and come and live here. We are much happier now. I love to study 20 plants and animals. My sister likes to do the same thing. We have books, we have our studies, and we have interesting neighbours. Dr Mortimer knows a great deal about medicine. Poor Sir Charles was also a very interesting person. We knew him well, and miss him 25 very much. By the way, do you think I should go and see Sir Henry this afternoon?'

'I am sure he would be glad to see you.'

'Then would you please tell him that I'll be coming. And now, please come upstairs, Dr Watson. I want you 30 to see my collection of butterflies. After that, we'll have lunch.'

But I wanted to get back to Baskerville Hall. I could not understand Miss Stapleton's warning, but I was worried for Sir Henry. I told Stapleton that I could not 35 stay for lunch. I walked straight back to the Hall.

Watson's first report

A few days later, I sent a report to Holmes.

Baskerville Hall, 13th October.
My dear Holmes,

I have told you everything about this place in my   5
earlier letters and telegrams, but I have not said much
about the escaped prisoner. I think he has got away.
He escaped from prison about two weeks ago. Nobody
has seen him since. He can hide easily on the moor,
but there is nothing for him to eat. The farmers are   10
worried that he will catch one of their sheep for food.
But most people think he has gone away from the
moor.

Sir Henry Baskerville seems to like Miss Stapleton.
This is not surprising. She is a very beautiful woman.   15
But she is very much afraid of her brother. When she
talks, she keeps looking at him. She seems afraid that
her brother might not like what she is saying.

Stapleton himself is a strange fellow. He came to visit
Sir Henry on the first day. The next morning, he took   20
us to a valley where people say that Hugo Baskerville
met the hound. It is some miles away across the moor.
In the middle of the valley, there are two big stones.
They look like the teeth of a large animal. It is a
frightening place. Sir Henry was very interested. He   25
asked Stapleton several times whether he believed in
the supernatural. Stapleton was very careful in his
answers. He did not tell Sir Henry everything he knew.

On our way back, we had lunch at Merripit House.
That was when Sir Henry met Miss Stapleton for the   30
first time. As we walked back, he talked about her many
times. Since then, we have seen the Stapletons every
day. They will be coming for dinner at the Hall tonight.
We will be going to their house next week.

I thought Stapleton would be happy with the friendship between Sir Henry and his sister. As a brother, he should want his sister to marry a rich man. But this does not seem to be so. Several times I saw a
5 displeased look on his face. He must love her very much. Of course, he would be very lonely without her.

On Thursday, Dr Mortimer visited us. The Stapletons came later. Sir Henry asked the doctor to show us the Yew Alley. He wanted to know how Sir Charles
10 Baskerville died.

The Alley is a long, straight path with tall hedges on each side. There is an old summer-house at the far end. The moor gate is half-way down. This is where Sir Charles dropped his cigar-ash. The moor is just outside
15 the Alley.

I remember what you said about the whole thing. You said Sir Charles was standing in the Alley. Then he saw something on the moor which frightened him. So he ran. He was very frightened and excited. That was
20 why he died. But what did he run from? A sheep-dog? Or a ghostly hound?

I have just met a neighbour named Mr Frankland. He lives in Lafter Hall, about four miles away. He is quite an old man, with a red face and white hair. He likes to
25 study the stars and he owns a very good telescope which he keeps on the roof of his house. At present he uses the telescope every day to look for the escaped prisoner on the moor.

There is one other thing I want to tell you in this
30 report. Last night, about two in the morning, I was woken by the sound of soft footsteps outside my room. I got up, opened my door, and looked out.

I could see a long black shadow. A man was walking down the corridor, holding a candle in his hand. It was
35 Barrymore. He was walking very slowly and quietly.

I waited until he had gone out of sight, then I followed him. I could not see him, but I could see the light of the candle through an open door. He had entered one of the rooms. All the rooms in this part of the house are empty. Nobody stays in them. I looked around the door.

Barrymore was standing near the window. He was holding the candle close to the glass. I could see the side of his face. He seemed to be looking for something outside. For some minutes, he stood there looking towards the moor. Then he put out his light.

I went back to my room quickly. I heard his footsteps passing by outside. Later, I heard a key being turned in a lock. I could not tell where the sound came from.

I do not know what this is all about. But something secret is happening in this house.

STRANGE BEHAVIOUR

Watson's second report

Baskerville Hall, 15th October

My dear Holmes,

I have a few things to tell you in this report which
will surprise you.

I went into the room where Barrymore had gone in
the middle of the night, and I examined the window
where he had stood. It looks out on to the moor.
Barrymore must have been looking for something or
somebody outside.

I also spoke to Sir Henry about what I had seen. He
did not seem surprised. He said that he knew
Barrymore walked about the house at night. We
decided that next time we would follow him to see
what he was looking for.

Later Sir Henry said he was going to meet Miss
Stapleton. He said he wanted to be alone with her, and
so he did not want me to go with him. I felt very uneasy
when he had left. Whatever his excuse was, I should
not have let him go alone. He might meet with danger
on the way. So I decided to follow him. I set off at once
towards Merripit House.

I walked very fast, but I could not see Sir Henry at
all. I feared I had gone in the wrong direction. So I
climbed a little hill from where I could look all round.
I saw him at once.

He was about a quarter of a mile away, and Miss
Stapleton was by his side. It was clear that the two of
them had agreed to meet there.

They were walking slowly, and talking at the same time. Miss Stapleton was talking in an excited way. She made quick little movements with her hands. Sir Henry was listening quietly. Once or twice he shook his head as if he disagreed with what she said. I stood among the rocks, watching them.

Then Sir Henry and the lady stopped. Suddenly I saw another person watching them. It was Stapleton. He was nearer them than I was. He seemed to be moving towards them.

Stapleton's anger

Sir Henry suddenly pulled Miss Stapleton towards his side. He put his arm around her. She seemed to be pulling away from him. Then suddenly they both stepped back from each other. They had seen Stapleton.

Stapleton ran towards them, and the two men talked for some minutes. The lady stood by quietly. She did not seem to like Stapleton's behaviour. Finally, Stapleton turned away angrily. He called to his sister to follow him. She looked at Baskerville for a moment, and then she followed her brother. Sir Henry began to walk slowly back towards Baskerville Hall. He looked very sad.

I ran down the hill and met Sir Henry at the bottom. He was surprised when he saw me. I explained to him why I had decided to follow him. I also told him I had seen everything. At first, he was quite angry. Then he laughed. He was surprised by my honesty.

Sir Henry said that he could not understand why Stapleton seemed to hate him so much. He said he was very much in love with Miss Stapleton, and he thought she loved him too. But they had not been talking about love. She had kept telling him that this was a place of danger for him. She wanted him to go away from the

moor, and to leave Baskerville Hall. Sir Henry had told
her that he did not want to leave because of her. He
had asked her to marry him.

'But before she could answer me, her brother
appeared,' said Sir Henry. 'He was like a madman, and
very angry.

'I told him that I loved his sister, and hoped to
marry her. That seemed to make him even more angry.
I lost my temper too. I shouted back at him. Then he
went off with his sister. I still do not understand his
behaviour. Just tell me what it all means, Watson.'

I did not understand it myself. However, that
afternoon, Stapleton came to explain everything. He
said he was very sorry for his behaviour that morning.
He had a long talk with Sir Henry alone. He explained
to Sir Henry that he was a very lonely man. His only
companion was his sister, so he was afraid of losing
her. He said that he had been
shocked to find out that
Sir Henry loved his
sister. That was why
he had behaved so
foolishly.

They became quite friendly after that. Stapleton invited both of us to dinner at Merripit House next Friday.

So, the reasons for Stapleton's strange behaviour are now quite clear. 5

Mrs Barrymore tells the truth

Now there was another problem to think about. This was Barrymore's behaviour.

On the night of Stapleton's visit, Sir Henry and I decided to stay awake in Sir Henry's room. We did not 10 hear anything until three o'clock in the morning. Then somebody walked quietly past the door. Baskerville quickly opened the door and we both went out into the corridor, following the sound of the footsteps.

The corridor was dark. We could not see anybody. 15 We walked quietly to the far side of Baskerville Hall. We were just in time to see a tall man with a black beard, carrying a candle.

Barrymore went into the same room as before. We moved slowly towards the open door. When we looked 20 in, we saw him at the same window, looking out at the moor.

Sir Henry walked into the room and Barrymore sprang back from the window, looking very frightened. Sir Henry asked him what he was doing. Barrymore did 25 not want to explain, but Sir Henry became angry and said that if he would not tell him the truth he and his wife would have to stop working at Baskerville Hall. At that moment Mrs Barrymore came in.

'Oh, John, John,' she said, 'what have I done to you? 30 It is my fault, Sir Henry, all mine. He did it because of me. I asked him to.'

'Speak out, then! What does it mean?'

'It's my brother. He is dying of hunger on the moor.
We cannot let him die at our very gates. I prepare food
for him. That light outside marks the place where we
must take the food.' Mrs Barrymore pointed out of the
window. We could see a tiny light outside.

'Then your brother is …'

'The escaped prisoner, sir — Selden the criminal.'

'That's the truth, sir,' said Barrymore. 'It was not my
secret. I could not tell it to you. But now you have
heard it, sir. There is no plan of any kind against you.'

Sir Henry and I both looked at the woman in great
surprise.

'Yes, sir, my name was Selden before I was married.
The escaped prisoner is my younger brother. We spoilt
him when he was a boy. We let him do everything he
liked. Then, as he grew older, he met with bad
companions. He did one wrong thing after another. But
I still love my brother.

'When he escaped from prison he came here. He
knew I was staying here and that I would help him.
Barrymore and I gave him food and took care of
him.

'Then you came from London, sir. My brother
decided to hide on the moor. He would stay there until
the soldiers stopped looking for him. Once every two
nights, we would put a light by the window. If Selden
was still there, he would answer us. Then my husband
would take some food out to him. Every day, we hoped
that he would go away. But as long as he is there, we
must help him.'

'Is this true, Barrymore?'

'Yes, Sir Henry.'

'Well, I cannot blame you. You have to help your
own wife. Go to your room, you two. We shall talk
about this matter in the morning.'

Hunting for a criminal

When they were gone, we looked out of the window again. We could see a small light, on a nearby hillside. Sir Henry said we should try to catch the prisoner while we knew where he was. If we waited too long he would put out the light and go away.

We were ready to go out in five minutes. It was very dark outside. Just as we reached the moor, a little rain began to fall. We could still see the light in front of us. Slowly we went closer. At last we could see a person sitting by the light.

Suddenly we heard a strange cry. It was the same cry which I had heard on Grimpen Mire. It began with a low sound. Then it became a howl, like the sound a wolf makes, and slowly died away. Again and again we heard it. Sir Henry caught hold of my sleeve. His face was white.

'Good heavens, what's that, Watson?'

'I don't know. It's quite often heard on the moor. I have heard it once before.'

The sound died away again. Then there was silence.

'Watson,' said Sir Henry, 'I am sure it was the cry of a hound.'

Baskerville had become very frightened. He could hardly speak. I too became frightened when I saw him like this.

I took his arm and led him towards the criminal's light. It was still burning brightly before us.

The criminal was gone. He must have been frightened by the strange cry, too. We rushed to the top of the hill and saw him running down on the other side.

Sir Henry and I were both good runners. We began to chase the man, but he got farther and farther away. We would never catch him. We stopped running and decided to go home. Then a very strange thing happened.

I saw someone on the hill top. It was very dark, but I was sure I saw a tall thin man standing there with his legs apart, his arms folded, and his head bowed.

It was not the escaped prisoner. This man was far from the place where the criminal had gone. And he was a much taller man. With a cry of surprise, I pointed him out to Sir Henry, but suddenly the man was gone. We could not see him any more.

Sir Henry said the man might be a prison officer and that is probably the correct explanation. But I would like to be more certain about it.

You must agree, Holmes, that I have given you plenty of facts to think about. Much of what I have written is probably unimportant, but I thought I should tell you everything, and let you decide what is useful and what is not.

From Dr Watson's Diary

Barrymore's complaint

At this point in my story, I will take some passages from my diary. I will start with the morning after the night we chased the escaped prisoner.

October 16th — It is a grey, foggy day, with light rain. Sir Henry is still feeling shocked after what happened last night. I am feeling uneasy myself. I feel as though something dangerous will soon take place.

Everything that has happened shows that there is evil around this place. Sir Charles died in a very strange way. The people on the moor say that they have seen a strange creature many times. I myself have heard the strange sound. It is very much like the cry of a hound.

There were also the things which happened in London — the warning letter to Sir Henry, and the missing boot. The warning might be the work of a friend or an enemy. Where is that person now? Is he still in London, or has he followed us down here? Could he be the stranger I saw on the hill top?

I only had one look at the stranger, but I am sure of one thing. I have never seen him before in this place. He was very much taller than Stapleton, and thinner than Frankland. It might have been Barrymore, but we left him behind us at the Hall, and I am sure he could not have followed us.

In London, a stranger had been following Sir Henry and Dr Mortimer. Now a stranger is following us here. I feel sure that if we could find this man, we would learn many things. I must now do everything I can to find him.

After breakfast this morning, Barrymore wanted to speak to Sir Henry. They went to his study. After some time, Sir Henry opened his door and called for me.

'Barrymore has a complaint to make,' he said. 'He
5 thinks that it was unfair of us to try to catch his brother-in-law.'

The butler was standing before us. He was very pale but calm.

'Look, Barrymore,' said Sir Henry, 'that man is very
10 dangerous. We had to try to catch him. There are lonely houses all over the moor. He might harm the people there. Nobody is safe until he is caught.'

'He'll not break into any house, sir. I can promise you this. And he will not trouble anyone again in this
15 country. In a few days the poor fellow will be on a ship going to South America. Sir Henry, I beg you. Please don't tell the police where he is. They have stopped looking for him. He can wait quietly until the ship is ready.'

20 'What do you think, Watson?'

'If he leaves the country, it's all right then,' I replied.

'But what if he robs someone before he goes?'

'He would not do anything so mad, sir. The police would then know where he is hiding.'

25 'That is true,' said Sir Henry. 'Well, Barrymore — '

'I cannot thank you enough, sir. If he were caught again, my wife would be heart-broken.'

'All right, Barrymore, you can go.'

The letter

30 The man was very grateful.

'You have been so kind to us, sir. I should like to do something to help you. There is something which I found out after the inquest. I have not told it to anybody yet. It's about poor Sir Charles's death.'

Sir Henry and I both jumped to our feet in surprise.
'What is it?' we cried.

'I know why he was at the gate at that hour. It was
to meet a woman.'

'What is the woman's name?'

'I can't give you the name, sir, but I can give you the
initials. Her initials were L.L.'

'How do you know this, Barrymore?'

'Well, Sir Henry, on that morning, a letter came for
your uncle. It was the only one, so I remember it very
well. It was from Coombe Tracey. The address on the
envelope was written in a woman's handwriting.'

'Well?'

'Well, sir, after I had given it to Sir Charles I did not
think any more about it. Then, a few weeks ago my
wife was cleaning Sir Charles's study. Nobody had been
in there since his death. She found the ashes of a burnt
letter in the fireplace. But the letter was not completely
burnt. The end of one page was still there. The writing
on it could be read clearly. It looked like a note at the
end of the letter, and it said:
"Please, please, burn this
letter and be at the gate
by ten o'clock — L.L." '

'Have you got that piece of the letter?'

'No, sir, it fell to pieces when we moved it.'

'Had Sir Charles received any other letters in the same writing?'

5 'Well, sir, I did not usually look at his letters. I remembered this one because it was the only one that came on the day that Sir Charles died.'

'And you don't know who L.L. is?'

'Not at all, sir. If we can find this lady, we should 10 know more about Sir Charles's death.'

'Why didn't you say anything about this letter before, Barrymore?'

'Well, sir, after I found out about the letter, my brother-in-law came, and then I forgot all about it. But 15 now you have been kind to us, sir. So I had to tell you about it.'

When the butler had left us, Sir Henry turned to me. 'What do you think of this, Watson?'

'It makes everything more difficult to understand.'

20 'I think so, too. But if we can find L.L., we should know everything. What do you think we should do?'

'Let us tell Holmes what we have learned. He will know what to do. I think he will come here now.'

I went up to my room and wrote a report to Holmes. 25 I knew Holmes was very busy. He had only written to me a few times, and his letters were very short. But I knew the things which had happened in the past few days would interest him very much.

I wish he were here right now.

30 Frankland's daughter

October 17th — It rained without stopping the whole day. I thought of the escaped prisoner on the cold moor outside. Poor fellow! He is being punished for his crimes. And then I thought of the other person — the person on the hilltop. Was he also out there in the rain — the unseen watcher?

In the evening I put on my raincoat and went out on to the moor. It was still raining, and a strong wind was blowing. I came to Black Tor, the hilltop where I had seen the unknown person. There was nobody there.

As I walked back, Dr Mortimer drove by in his carriage. He gave me a ride home.

'By the way, Dr Mortimer,' I said, 'do you know everybody here?'

'More or less, I think.'

'Can you tell me the name of a woman whose initials are L.L.?'

He thought for a few minutes. 'Yes, there is Laura Lyons — her initials are L.L. — but she lives in Coombe Tracey.'

'Who is she?' I asked.

'She is Frankland's daughter. She married an artist named Lyons. But they were not happy together. The man treated her very badly, and after a while he left her. Old Frankland did not want his daughter back with him. You see, she married against his wishes.'

'How does she live?'

'I think the father gives her a bit of money. It cannot be much. He has too many of his own things to take care of. Several of us tried to help her. We tried to get her some work. Stapleton, Sir Charles and I gave her some money to start a typewriting business.'

Dr Mortimer wanted to know why I was asking him these questions. I did not tell him everything. Tomorrow morning I shall go to Coombe Tracey. If I can see this Mrs Laura Lyons, I might learn something.

THE MAN ON BLACK TOR

At Coombe Tracey

At breakfast the next morning I told Sir Henry what I had learnt from Dr Mortimer. I asked him to go with me to Coombe Tracey to see Mrs Lyons. At first, he
5 wanted to come very much. Then we both thought it would be better if I went alone. I would learn more this way.

When I reached Coombe Tracey, I easily found the place where Mrs Lyons lived. A servant showed me in.
10 Mrs Lyons was sitting in front of a typewriter. She got up with a smile. But when she saw that I was a stranger, she sat down again. She asked me the purpose of my visit.

I told her my name, and said that I knew her father.
15 'I have nothing to do with my father,' she said. 'His friends are not friends of mine. He does not care for me at all. It was Sir Charles Baskerville and a few other people who helped me.'

'It is about Sir Charles Baskerville that I have come
20 to see you. I want to ask you if you ever wrote to Sir Charles.'

She was silent and her face was very pale. Then she looked up.

'I wrote to him once or twice to thank him for his
25 kindness.'

'Do you remember the dates of those letters?'

'No.'

'Did you ever meet him?'

'Yes, once or twice, when he came to Coombe
30 Tracey.'

'You seldom saw him, and you seldom wrote to him. Then why did he help you? He must have known you well.'

'There were several gentlemen who knew about what happened to me. They got together to help me. One was Mr Stapleton, a neighbour and close friend of Sir Charles. He was very kind. Sir Charles learnt about me from him.'

'Did you ever write to Sir Charles asking him to meet you?' I continued.

Mrs Lyons became angry again.

'Really, sir, that is a very strange question.'

'I am sorry, Madam, but I must ask you about it.'

'Then I will answer — certainly not.'

'Not on the day when Sir Charles died?' She became very uneasy.

'You must remember it,' I continued. 'I can tell you part of your letter. It read: "Please, please, burn this letter, and be at the gate by ten o'clock."'

She almost fainted when she heard this.

'I thought I could trust Sir Charles,' she said.

'Sir Charles did burn the letter. But a part of it was left behind. Did you write that letter?'

'Yes, I did write it,' she replied. 'I did write it. Why should I say I didn't? I am not ashamed of it. I wanted his help. That was why I asked him to meet me.'

'But why at such a time?'

'Because I had just learned that he was going to London the next day. He would not be back for many months. It is a long way to Baskerville Hall, and I could not get there earlier.'

'And why did you ask him to meet you in the garden, instead of inside the house?'

'Surely you do not think it would be right for me to meet an unmarried man in his house so late in the evening!'

'Well, what happened
when you did get there?'

'I never went.'

'Mrs Lyons, tell me
5 the truth!'

'It's true! I never went.
Something happened,
and I could not go.'

'What happened?'

10 'It's my own
business. I cannot
tell you.'

'You asked him
to meet you at the
15 time and place where
he died, but you didn't go.
That is rather hard to believe.'

'It is the truth.'

I asked her a few other questions, but she did not
20 want to tell me anything more.

'Mrs Lyons,' I said, 'I am sure that you have not told
me everything you know. If I tell the police about this,
you will be in trouble. Why did you ask Sir Charles to
burn that letter?'

25 'All right, I'll tell you. I think you know that my
married life was very unhappy. I found out I could
divorce my husband only if I paid him some money.
And I wanted very much to be free of him. I knew Sir
Charles was a very generous person. He would have
30 helped me if I had gone to see him.'

'Then why didn't you go?'

'Because on the same day that I had arranged to meet
Sir Charles, I was able to get all the help I needed from
another person.'

35 'Why didn't you tell this to Sir Charles?'

'I wanted to, but by then it was too late to go to Baskerville Hall. Then, the next morning, I read about his death in the newspaper.'

I believed the woman's story. It seemed to be true. I could find out if she had been trying to divorce her husband at the time Sir Charles died. I could also find out if she had been to Baskerville Hall. She would have had to take a carriage. The journey from Coombe Tracey would have taken several hours. She would not have been able to return till the early morning. Many people would have known about a journey like that. It could not have been kept a secret.

She must have been telling me the truth, or part of the truth. I was very puzzled when I left her house. I still felt that Mrs Lyons had not told me everything.

I thought of the man I had seen on the hill top of Black Tor. If I could find him, I would learn many things. There were some empty huts on the moor, and I decided to search for him there. He should be in one of them. If I found him, I would use my gun to make him talk. If he were not in the huts, I would wait for him.

Frankland's discovery

On the way home, I met Mr Frankland. He was standing outside his garden gate.

'Good day, Dr Watson,' he said. He seemed to be very happy. 'You must give your horses a rest here. Come in and have a glass of wine with me.'

I did not like the way he had treated his daughter, so I did not feel very friendly towards him. But I decided to accept his invitation. I told the driver to take the carriage to Baskerville Hall, and I followed Mr Frankland into his house.

'It's about the escaped prisoner,' he told me, laughing. 'I do not know exactly where he is. But I do know where to look for him. Do you know the best way of catching a man? Find out where he gets his food.'

5   I became worried. 'But are you certain he is still on the moor?'

'I have seen the person who takes him his food.'

I became worried for Barrymore. Frankland might get him into trouble. But his next words made me less
10 worried.

'You'll be surprised to hear that his food is taken to him by a boy. I see him every day through my telescope on the roof. He goes along the same path at the same hour.'

15 I knew that the boy could not be taking food to the prisoner. Barrymore took him his food only at night. Frankland must have discovered the stranger's hiding place.

'Perhaps it is just the son of one of the shepherds
20 taking food to his father,' I suggested.

'Indeed, sir!' he said. 'The boy goes to the stoniest part of the whole moor. A shepherd would never take his sheep there.'

I said that I had spoken without knowing all the facts.
25 This pleased him.

'You may be sure, sir, that I have thought about the whole matter very carefully. I have seen the boy again and again with his bag, every day, and sometimes twice a day. I have been able ... but wait a minute, Dr Watson!
30 There is something on the hillside right now!'

Several miles away, I could see something moving slowly up the hillside.

'Come, sir, come!' cried Frankland, rushing upstairs to the roof of his house. 'You will see this with your
35 own eyes.'

Frankland put his eye to the telescope, and gave a cry of satisfaction.

'Quick, Dr Watson, quick, before he passes over the hill!'

Through the telescope, I could see a boy slowly   5
going up the hill. Then he reached the top and went down the other side. He could not be seen any more.

'Well! Am I right?'

'Certainly. There is a boy who seems to be doing something secret.'   10

'What he is doing is very clear. Even a village policeman would be able to guess. But I am not going to tell them anything. They have never helped me, and I am not going to help them. You must promise me that you will not tell them either. Not a word! You understand?'

'Just as you wish.'

Waiting for the stranger

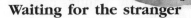

After some time, I left Mr Frankland's house. I walked towards Baskerville Hall till he could not see me any more. Then I cut back across the moor. I went straight for the hill where the boy had been.   25

The sun was already setting when I reached the top. I could not see or hear anybody moving about. The boy had gone.

There was a circle of stone huts below. One of them still had a good roof. I became excited when I saw it.   30
That must be where the stranger was living.

I threw away the cigarette I had been smoking, and walked slowly towards the hut. The stranger might be there now. I took out my gun and then, moving quickly to the door, looked in. The place was empty.

5   But it was certainly the place where the man lived. I could see the ashes of a fire. There were some pots for cooking and a bucket half-full of water.

On a flat stone lay some tins of food. Under them was a sheet of paper. There was some writing on it. I
10 picked up the paper. Written in pencil was the message: 'Dr Watson has gone to Coombe Tracey.'

I stood still for a minute with the paper in my hand. It was I, then, and not Sir Henry, who was being followed by this man. He had not followed me himself.
15 He must have got somebody else to do it for him. It could be the boy, and the paper was clearly the boy's report. Perhaps he had watched everything I had done since I came.

I guessed there would be other reports, so I searched
20 the hut for more pieces of paper. But I did not find anything. There was also nothing to show who the strange person was. I decided to stay and wait for him to come back.

The sun was already setting. I sat in the hut and
25 waited, feeling rather uneasy.

And then I heard him. From far away came the sounds of a boot hitting a stone. The person was coming nearer and nearer. I hid in a dark corner of the hut, and got my gun ready. There was a long silence.
30 The stranger must have stopped. Then, once more, the footsteps came nearer, and then stopped again. A shadow fell across the opening of the hut.

'It's such a lovely evening, my dear Watson,' said a well-known voice. 'I think you should come outside.
35 It's more comfortable out here.'

DEATH ON THE MOOR

I could hardly believe what I had heard. I easily
recognized that sharp voice.

'Holmes!' I cried. 'Holmes!'

'Come out,' he said, 'and please be careful with that
gun.' 5

I stood at the doorway. There he sat upon a stone
outside. He seemed amused at my surprise.

'I am very, very glad to see you,' I said.

'And surprised, eh?'

'Well, I must say I am.' 10

'I am also surprised, Watson. I did not think you
would find out about this hut. I did not know you were
inside until I came near. I saw the burnt end of your
cigarette on the ground. Very few people here smoke
that kind of cigarette. So I knew you were around. Did 15
you think I was the criminal?'

'I did not know who you were.'

'Good, Watson! And how did you find me? You must
have seen me on the night you chased the escaped
prisoner. I made a mistake that time. I stood on the 20
hilltop with the moon rising behind me.'

'Yes, I saw you that night. Your boy was also seen.
I followed him here.'

'Ah, the old gentleman with his telescope must have
noticed him.' 25

He rose and looked into the hut.

'I see that young Cartwright has brought me some
food. He came from London with me. He gets me all
the things I need here. What's this? Oh, so you have
been to Coombe Tracey? To see Mrs Laura Lyons?' 30

'Yes.'

'Well done! We have each been looking for the same things. When we put our answers together, we will know a lot about this case.'

'Well, I am glad that you are here. I feel I cannot do
5   everything by myself. But how did you get here? What have you been doing? I thought you were working in Baker Street.'

'I wanted you to think that.'

'Then you did not trust me!' I cried, rather angrily.
10 'You did not think I could work here alone.'

'My dear fellow, you have been very helpful to me in this case. It is true, I have played a trick on you, and please forgive me for this. But I came to Dartmoor because I wanted to look at the case myself. I did not
15 want to be with you and Sir Henry. We would all have been finding the same answers then. Also I did not want Sir Henry's enemies to know I was here. It would have made them very careful.'

'Then my reports have all been wasted!' I became
20 angry with Holmes. I had taken so much trouble in writing those reports.

Holmes took a bundle of papers from his pocket.

'Here are your reports, my dear fellow. I have read them very carefully. I had them sent to me. They were very well written, Watson. And now, you must tell me the result of your visit to Mrs Laura Lyons.

I guess you went to Coombe Tracey to see her. She is
the only person there who can help us.'

I told Holmes of my meeting with the lady.

Stapleton is the enemy

'This is most important,' said he, when I had finished.
'It tells us something which we did not know. And you
have discovered, I suppose, that Mrs Lyons and
Stapleton are good friends?'

'No.'

'I am very sure of it. They meet and they write to
each other. They know each other very well. If I tell
Stapleton's wife about it, she will be willing to help us.'

'His wife?'

'I will tell you now what I have learnt. Miss Stapleton
is not Stapleton's sister. She is his wife.'

'Good heavens, Holmes! Are you sure of what you
say? But why does he lie about her?'

'Because he wants to use her. She is a beautiful
woman. If she were not married, many men would fall
in love with her.'

'It is he, then, who is our enemy. It is he who
followed us in London?'

'I think so.'

'And the warning — it must have come from her!'

'Yes.'

'But are you sure of this, Holmes? How do you know
that the woman is his wife?'

'When he first met you, he told you something about
himself which is true. He said he once had a school in
the north of England. I checked up on this. It is very
easy to find out about schools. I soon heard of one
that had closed down at about the right time. The
schoolmaster and his wife had disappeared. The names
were different, but both Stapleton and the missing

schoolmaster love to collect butterflies and insects, so I am sure they are the same person.'

'If this woman is his wife, what about Mrs Laura Lyons?' I asked.

'Mrs Lyons has told you that she was going to divorce her husband. She must be thinking of marrying Stapleton. After all, nobody here knows he is already married.'

'What happens when she finds out?'

'Why, then she will be very willing to help us. We will go and see her tomorrow. Right now, you must go back to Baskerville Hall. You have left Sir Henry alone for a long time.'

The sun had already set. It was dark on the moor.

'One last question, Holmes,' I said as I rose. 'What is Stapleton trying to do?'

Holmes answered in a very low voice. 'Murder, Watson. I can't tell you everything now. He is planning to kill Sir Henry. I want to get him before anything serious happens, and I need your help, but he must act first before we can do anything. I think it will all be over very soon. Until then, you must guard Sir Henry very carefully. But what was that?'

A terrible scream was heard on the moor. It was a frightening cry.

'Oh, my God,' I said. 'What is it?'

The scream was heard a second time. It was louder and nearer.

'There, I think.' I pointed into the darkness.

'No, there!'

The frightening cry was heard once more. It was much louder and much nearer. Then there was another. But this time it was the deep, angry cry of a hound.

'The hound!' cried Holmes. 'Come, Watson, come. My God! I hope we are not too late!'

'I should not have left him alone!'

He ran quickly over the moor. I followed him closely. Then, from in front of us, we heard one last cry, and the sound of something falling. We stopped and listened. There was only silence.   5

Holmes looked very unhappy.

'He has beaten us, Watson. I should have stopped him. And you, Watson, should not have left Baskerville alone. But if he is dead, we will get his killer.'

We ran on in the direction of the cries we had heard.   10 It was very dark. Then we heard a low cry of pain. It came from a steep slope. As we went nearer, we saw a dark object lying on the ground.

It was a man. He was facing downwards, with his head under his body. It was clear that his neck was   15 broken. Holmes lit a match and cried out. In front of him was the body of Sir Henry Baskerville!

We recognized the clothes. Sir Henry had worn them when we first saw him in Baker Street.

'That animal! That animal!' I cried in anger. 'Oh,   20 Holmes, I can never forgive myself! I should not have left him alone!'

'It's more my fault, Watson. I could have saved Sir Henry, but I wanted to catch Stapleton. I waited too long. I will never be able to forget my mistake. But why did Sir Henry come to the moor alone? I warned him not to do this!'

We felt very angry with ourselves. We had let a man die. All our work was now wasted.

'What can we do?' I asked sadly.

'We have many things to do tomorrow. Tonight we have to get ready for our friend's funeral.'

'We must send for help, Holmes! We cannot carry him all the way to the Hall.'

Holmes suddenly gave a cry and bent over the body. Then he jumped for joy and began to laugh.

'Good heavens, are you mad, Holmes?'

'A beard! A beard! This man has a beard!'

'A beard?'

'Look, this is not Sir Henry! Why, it is the escaped prisoner! He must have been living in these huts near me all the time.'

Then I remembered that Sir Henry had told me he had given some of his old clothes to Barrymore. The butler must have given them to Selden to help him escape. The boots, shirt and hat worn by the prisoner had all belonged to Sir Henry. I told Holmes what I knew.

'Then these clothes were the cause of his death,' he said. 'It is clear that the hound was given something belonging to Sir Henry to smell. It must have been that boot Sir Henry lost in the hotel. So the hound must have followed Sir Henry's smell from these clothes. My work now is to catch the man who frightened Sir Charles to death, and who is trying to kill Sir Henry. But, who's this coming?'

Somebody was walking quickly towards us over the moor. He stopped when he saw us. Then he came closer.

'Why, it's Stapleton himself! ' said Holmes. 'Don't tell him what we know about him, Watson, otherwise my plan will fail.'

Stapleton is surprised

'Why, Dr Watson, it is you! I did not expect to see you here on the moor at this time of night. But, dear me, what's this? Is somebody hurt? Don't tell me it is Sir Henry?' 5

Quickly, he went to look at the dead man. I could see that he was surprised.

'Who … who's this?' he asked.

'It is Selden, the man who escaped from Princetown.'

There was an ugly look on Stapleton's face when he 10 heard this. He looked at both Holmes and me. Then he quickly hid his surprise.

'Dear me! What a frightening thing! How did he die?'

'He broke his neck by falling over those rocks. My friend and I were walking on the moor when we heard 15 a cry.'

'I heard the cry too. That was why I came here. I was worried about Sir Henry.'

'Why Sir Henry?' I asked.

'Because I had asked him to come to my house. I 20 was surprised when he did not come. I was worried for his safety when I heard the cries. By the way, did you hear anything else?' He looked at Holmes and me when he asked this.

'No,' said Holmes.

'Did you?'

'No.'

'Why did you ask then?'

'Oh, you know the stories about a strange hound. The farmers here say it is heard at night upon the moor. I thought you might have heard something tonight.'

'We heard nothing like that,' I said.

'Why do you think this fellow died?' he asked.

'I think he became mad after staying on the moor for so long. He did not know what he was doing. So he fell and broke his neck,' I replied.

'That may be true,' said Stapleton. He seemed to be pleased with my answer. 'What do you think about it, Mr Sherlock Holmes?'

Holmes bowed. 'You are very clever to recognize me so quickly.'

'We have been expecting you since Dr Watson came to stay at Baskerville Hall. You have come in time to see something very sad.'

'Yes indeed. I shall take an unpleasant memory back to London with me tomorrow.'

'Oh, you return tomorrow?'

'Yes.'

'I hope you have found out something about the strange things that have been happening here.'

'I cannot always be successful, you know. There are too many legends in this case, and not enough facts. I am not at all happy about it.'

Holmes spoke as if he was being very truthful. Stapleton looked hard at him. Then he turned to me.

'I thought of carrying this poor fellow to my house. But my sister would be frightened if she saw him. I think we'll put something over his face and leave him here till the morning.'

After doing this, Holmes and I set off for Baskerville Hall. Stapleton went home alone. He had asked us to go with him to his house. We politely refused.

11

SETTING THE TRAP

Nothing can be proved

Holmes and I walked together across the moor.

'We are getting somewhere at last,' said Holmes. 'That fellow really surprises me! He must have been shocked that he had killed the wrong man, but he did not show it at all. I told you in London, Watson, and I tell you again now, Stapleton is a very clever enemy.'

'Stapleton knows you are here now. Do you think he will change his plans?'

'It may make him more careful. Or he may try to finish everything now. He thinks he has completely tricked us.'

'Why don't we arrest him at once?'

'My dear Watson, how can we arrest him? We cannot prove that he has done anything wrong. He is very clever, using that dog. It will not be easy to catch its master.'

'Surely we can prove that he has something to do with these deaths?'

'At present we cannot prove anything. We are just guessing.'

'What about Sir Charles's death?'

'He was found without a mark on him. We both know that he was frightened to death. We also know what frightened him. But how are we going to prove it? There was nothing to show that he was killed by a hound. There were no marks of its teeth. We know that a hound does not bite a dead body. Sir Charles was dead when the animal reached him. But how do we prove all this?'

'What about Selden's death?'

'Still nothing can be proved. There is nothing to show that a hound caused Selden's death. We never saw the hound. We heard it, but we cannot prove that it was running after this man. Anyway, Stapleton had no reason to kill Selden. Nobody would believe that he killed the man. No, my dear Watson, we cannot prove anything at the moment.'

'What do we do now?'

'We'll tell Mrs Laura Lyons everything about Stapleton. When she knows she has been tricked, she will help us. I have my own plan as well.'

I could not learn anything more from Holmes. We soon reached Baskerville Hall.

'Are you coming in?' I asked.

'Yes, there is no more reason for me to hide on the moor. But one last word, Watson. Don't say anything about the hound to Sir Henry. Let him think that Selden fell and broke his neck. Sir Henry will have to be very brave. Is he visiting the Stapletons tomorrow night?'

'Yes, and so am I.'

'You must not go with him. Give some excuse. Tomorrow night, Sir Henry must go alone. But right now, let's see if we can have something to eat here.'

The picture

Sir Henry was surprised, but very pleased to see Sherlock Holmes. We told him about what had happened on the moor. We did not say anything about the hound. I also told Barrymore and his wife about Selden's death. Mrs Barrymore was sad, but her husband was relieved. Selden had been a big worry for him.

'But what about the case?' asked Sir Henry. 'Have you discovered anything? Watson and I have not been able to learn much.'

'I shall be able to explain to you before long. It is a very difficult case. I am still not sure about a few things. However, I shall know the answers soon.'

'Watson and I have heard the hound. So it is something real,' said Sir Henry. 'If you can catch that dog and put it on a chain, I shall believe you are the greatest detective of all time.'

'I shall, but I need your help,' said Holmes.

'I shall do whatever you tell me to.'

'Very good, but you must not ask me any questions. You will have to do what I say.'

'Just as you like.'

'Then I think we will soon know ...'

Holmes stopped suddenly. He was looking at something behind me.

'What is it?' we both cried.

Then he looked away. He seemed to be thinking.

'Excuse me,' he said, and waved his hand at a picture on the wall. 'That is a member of your family, I suppose?'

'Ah, he is the cause of all our trouble. That is the wicked Hugo, who started the Hound of the Baskervilles.'

Holmes did not say much more, but he kept looking at the picture of Hugo Baskerville.

Later, when Sir Henry had gone to his room, Holmes took me back to the dining-hall. He had a candle with him. We held the light near the picture of Hugo.

'Do you see anything?'

I looked closely at the picture.

'Is it like anyone you know?'

'He is a bit like Sir Henry.'

5 'A bit, perhaps. But wait a minute.'

He stood upon a chair, holding the light in his left hand. With his right hand, he covered the hat and hair of Hugo Baskerville in the picture.

'Good heavens!' I cried in surprise.

10 'Ha, you see it now.'

'It is very much like Stapleton.'

'Yes, Stapleton looks and behaves like Hugo Baskerville. That fellow belongs to the family.'

'He must be hoping to get Baskerville Hall and the 15 fortune after Sir Henry dies.'

'Correct. This picture explains why Stapleton is doing all these strange things.'

Holmes makes his plans

I was up early the next morning, but Holmes was up 20 even earlier. As I was dressing, I saw him coming into the house.

'We have many things to do today,' he said. 'The nets are all ready for our fish.'

'Have you been on the moor already?'

25 'I went to Grimpen village to send a report to Princetown about Selden's death.'

'What do we do next?'

'See Sir Henry. Ah, here he is, now!'

'Good morning, Holmes,' said Sir Henry. 'You look 30 like a general making his plans.'

'Are you supposed to dine with the Stapletons tonight?'

'Yes, I hope you will come too. They are very friendly people, and would be glad to see you.'

'I am afraid that Watson and I must go to London.'

'To London?'

'Yes, we have something to do there.'

Sir Henry looked unhappy.

'I thought you were going to help me. It is very lonely 5
here on the moor, you know.'

'My dear fellow, you must trust me. Do what I tell
you. Tell the Stapletons we have to go away. We hope
to return here very soon. Please remember to tell them
this.'   10

'And there is one more thing, Sir Henry! I wish you
to drive to Merripit House. When you get there, send
back your carriage. Tell them that you will walk home
after dinner.'

'Walk across the moor in the dark?'   15

'Yes.'

'But you yourself asked me not to go out on the moor
alone.'

'This time you may do it. You will be safe. I know
you are a brave man, Sir Henry. You must walk back   20
alone.'

'Then I will do it.'

'There is one very important thing. You must walk
straight along the path from Merripit House to
Baskerville Hall. Do not go anywhere else.'   25

'I will do just as you say.'

'Very good. We will leave immediately after breakfast.
We must reach London by the afternoon.'

At Coombe Tracey again

We said goodbye to our sad friend. Two hours later,   30
we were at the station of Coombe Tracey. A boy was
waiting for us there.

'Any orders, sir?' he asked.

'You will take this train to London, Cartwright. When you arrive, you will send a telegram to Sir Henry Baskerville. Send it in my name. In the telegram, tell Sir Henry I have left my note book at his house. Ask
5   him to post it to me at Baker Street.'

'Yes, sir.'

'And now go and ask at the station if there is a message for me.'

The boy returned with a telegram. It said:

10   'Message received. Coming down this afternoon. Arriving at five-forty. — Lestrade.'

Lestrade was a police detective in London. He knew Holmes quite well.

'I have asked him to come,' said Holmes. 'We may
15   need help. Now, Watson, we will go and see Mrs Lyons.'

By now, I knew what Holmes's plan was. He wanted Stapleton to think that we had gone. Sir Henry would mention to him the telegram which Cartwright would
20   send from London. This would make Stapleton believe that we had gone. But all the time, both of us would still be around.

When we reached her house, Mrs Lyons was in her office.

25   'I have come to find out about Sir Charles's death,' said Holmes. 'My friend, Dr Watson, has told me what you told him. There are also a few things you did not tell him.'

'What did I not tell him?' she asked angrily.

30   'You said you asked Sir Charles to wait for you at the gate at ten o'clock. He died at that time and place. Do you know how he died?'

'I don't know.'

'I shall be honest with you, Mrs Lyons. Sir Charles
35   did not die of a heart attack. He was murdered. We can

prove that your friend Stapleton had something to do with it. And also his wife!'

Mrs Lyons jumped up from her chair. 'His wife!' she cried.

'Yes, we know all about it. Beryl Stapleton is his wife, not his sister.'

Mrs Lyons sat down again. She was holding the arms of her chair. She was clearly shocked.

'His wife!' she said again. 'His wife! He is not a married man. Prove it to me! Prove it to me!' She looked very fierce.

'I will prove it,' said Holmes. He took out some papers from his pocket. 'Here is a photograph of them taken in the north of England four years ago. "Mr and Mrs Vandeleur" is written on the back. You can recognize him easily. If you have seen his "sister", you will also recognize her.

'I also have three letters written by people whom you can trust. The letters describe Mr and Mrs Vandeleur. At that time, they were both working at St Oliver's private school. They owned the school. Read the letters. You will find out who Mr and Mrs Vandeleur are.'

'He has lied to me!'

Mrs Lyons looked at the letters. Then she looked at us with anger in her eyes.

'Mr Holmes,' she said, 'this man said he would marry me. He asked me to divorce my husband. He has lied to me! And why? Why? I thought he was trying to help me. He was using me! Why should I protect him now! I will tell you everything. Ask me what you want! But please believe me when I say that I did not mean Sir Charles any harm. He was my kindest friend.'

'I believe you, Madam,' said Holmes. 'Now, tell me, did Stapleton ask you to send the letter?'

'He told me what to write.'

'He promised to marry you, and because of that you needed a divorce. Then he said Sir Charles would help you get the money for the lawyers?'

5 'Yes.'

'And after you had sent the letter, Stapleton asked you not to go and see Sir Charles.'

'He said that he would find the money himself. He told me he would be ashamed if I received money from another man. After all, he was going to marry me.'

'And after Sir Charles's death he asked you not to say anything to anyone about meeting him?'

'He did. He said the death was very strange. The police would want to ask me questions if they knew I had wanted to meet Sir Charles. Stapleton frightened me into keeping quiet.'

'But didn't you think that Stapleton was behaving strangely?'

She looked down. 'I would never have said anything if he had not lied to me.'

'I think you are very lucky, Mrs Lyons,' said Holmes. 'You knew something about what he was doing. He might have killed you. We must leave you now. We may come to see you again.'

That evening, Holmes and I waited for the train from London.

'Our case becomes clearer,' said Holmes. 'We shall soon know the whole story.'

The train came into the station, and a small strongly-built man got down. The three of us shook hands.

'Any news?' asked Lestrade.

'It's the biggest case we have had for years,' said Holmes. 'We still have two hours more. Let's go and have dinner first. You have never been to Dartmoor, Lestrade. I think you are going to enjoy the cool night air here.'

THE HOUND OF THE BASKERVILLES

Outside Merripit House

We drove through the darkness and soon reached Baskerville Hall. Holmes paid the driver and asked him to return to Coombe Tracey. Then all three of us walked in the moonlight across the moor. We came to the path to Merripit House.

'Are you armed, Lestrade?' asked Holmes.

The detective smiled. 'Of course! I always carry my gun with me.'

'Good! My friend and I are also prepared.'

'You haven't told me much about this case, Mr Holmes. What do we do now?'

'We will wait. That is Merripit House in front of us. It's the end of our journey. We must be very quiet now. Don't talk loudly.'

We moved slowly towards the house. Holmes stopped us when we were about two hundred yards away.

'This is near enough,' he said. 'We will hide behind these rocks.'

'Are we to wait here?'

'Yes, we will wait here. Lestrade, get behind this rock. Watson, you have been inside the house, so you know it well. Creep forward quietly and look in. But don't let anyone hear or see you!'

I walked softly along the path until I came to the window of the main room. Inside I could see Sir Henry and Stapleton sitting at a round table. Both of them were smoking cigars, and drinking coffee and wine. Sir Henry looked pale and worried.

As I watched them, Stapleton rose and left the room. Sir Henry remained inside. I heard the sound of a door opening, and then footsteps. Stapleton came out of the house and went to a small building in the garden. He opened the door with a key, and went in. Some strange sounds came from inside this building. Stapleton remained there for a few minutes. Then he came out and locked the door. He re-entered the house and joined Sir Henry. I crept quietly back to Holmes and Lestrade, and told them what I had seen.

'You say, Watson, that the lady is not there?' Holmes asked.

'No.'

'Where can she be, then?'

'I did not see any other lights in the house. I do not know where she can be.'

The hound

It began to get foggy over Grimpen Mire, and the fog was moving slowly towards us. The moon shone on it. It looked like a large, low cloud.

'It's coming towards us, Watson.'

'Is that bad?'

'Very bad. Sir Henry will be leaving very soon. It is already ten o'clock. He must come out before the fog reaches here. His life depends on it!'

The night was clear and fine above us, and for a while we could still see the house.

But the fog soon covered more than half of the moor. Then it began to cover the ground around the house, too, so that only the roof could be seen.

Holmes got down on his knees and put his ear against the ground.

'I think I hear him coming!' he said.

We heard Sir Henry's footsteps. The steps got louder. Then we saw him as he came out of the fog. He walked very close to where we were hiding. As he went on towards Baskerville Hall, he kept looking behind him. It was clear that he was feeling frightened.   5

'Shhh!' cried Holmes. 'Look out! It's coming!' I heard him get his gun ready.

We could hear something running towards us, but we could see nothing. It was still hidden in the fog. All three of us felt afraid. Then a large animal rushed out of the fog.

It was the hound!

Lestrade fell to the ground in fear.

It was the biggest hound we had ever seen. It was all black. Flames came out of its mouth, and its eyes were like fire. It was a very frightening animal.

The hound was running towards Sir Henry. When it passed us, Holmes and I fired our guns. The animal gave a loud cry but kept on running.

This made us less frightened. We knew then that we could hurt the animal. This meant that it was not   25 supernatural. It was something which we could kill.

We saw Sir Henry looking back. In the moonlight, his face was white, and his hands were raised. He was looking straight at the hound. We heard him screaming in fear.   30

Holmes jumped up and ran very fast after the hound. I followed him. We saw the animal jump on to Sir Henry. Both of them fell to the ground. Holmes shot the animal five times. With a loud cry, it rolled upon its back and died.   35

Sir Henry was still lying on the ground. He was not hurt by the animal, but he was badly shocked. Lestrade took out a small bottle of brandy and poured it into Sir Henry's mouth.

5   Sir Henry opened his eyes, looking very frightened. 'My God !' he whispered. 'What was it? What was it?'

'It's dead, whatever it was,' said Holmes. 'We've killed the "Hound of the Baskervilles". No more Baskervilles will ever have to worry about this ghost again!'

10   **Something more to do**

The animal was very much larger than any dog we had ever seen. It was almost as big and as heavy as a small lion. There was a sort of blue-coloured flame around its jaws and eyes.

15   'Phosphorus — the chemical that shines in the dark,' I said, after examining the animal closely.

'The phosphorus used has no smell at all,' said Holmes. 'Otherwise, it would have disturbed the dog's sense of smell. I am very sorry, Sir Henry, for this shock.
20   I did not know the hound would be so frightening. And the fog made it difficult for us.'

'You have saved my life.'

'Yes, but I put you in danger. Are you strong enough to stand?'

25   'Give me some more of that brandy and I will be all right. Now, please help me up. What are you going to do now?'

'We will have to leave you here. You won't be able to follow us. One of us will come back afterwards to
30   help you get to the Hall.'

Sir Henry tried to get up, but he was still feeling very weak. We helped him to a rock. He sat down and put his face in his hands.

'We must leave you now,' said Holmes. 'We still have something to do. We must go and catch our man. We have to hurry.'

Then the three of us left Sir Henry sitting on the moor.

'I don't think we will find him in the house,' said Holmes. 'He must have heard those shots. He will know that we are coming for him.'

'But we were quite far away when we fired our guns,' I said. 'And it is difficult to hear properly in the fog.'

'I think he is gone by now. I am sure he followed the hound from the house. That means he heard us. But we'll search the house to make sure.'

The front door was open, so we rushed in, and searched all the rooms. Stapleton was not there. However, we found one of the rooms upstairs locked.

'There's someone in here!' cried Lestrade. 'I can hear something. Open this door!'

There was a soft cry from inside the room. Holmes kicked the door open. The three of us rushed in with our guns ready.

But Stapleton was not inside. The room was full of glass cases containing Stapleton's collection of butterflies. And there was someone in the room, but so tied up and covered with sheets that we could not see who it was.

We untied the person and took off the sheets. It was Mrs Stapleton! She fainted.

Holmes poured some brandy into Mrs Stapleton's mouth. She opened her eyes.

'Is Sir Henry safe?' she asked. 'Has he escaped?'

'Yes.'

'And the hound?'

'It is dead.'

'Thank God! Thank God! Look!' she said, pulling up her sleeves. 'See how that man has treated me!'

There were marks on her arms. It was clear that Stapleton had been beating her. Then she began to cry.

'Tell us where we can find him, Madam,' said Holmes.

5   'There is only one place he can escape to,' she answered. 'There is an old building in the middle of Grimpen Mire. He kept his hound there. He has turned it into a hiding place. He would go there if he was in any trouble.'

10   The fog was still very thick outside the house. We would not be able to go after Stapleton until the weather improved. We left Lestrade in the house with Mrs Stapleton. Holmes and I took Sir Henry back to Baskerville Hall.

15   We told Sir Henry everything that had happened. He was shocked to hear the truth about Mrs Stapleton. He had been very much in love with her.

The next morning, the fog was gone. Mrs Stapleton led us to her husband's hiding place in the middle of the Mire.

20   She did not go with us all the way. We left her behind at the edge of the Mire. From there, we followed little sticks stuck into the ground. Stapleton had placed them there to show the way through.

Along the way we saw a small dark object on the

25   ground. Holmes picked it up. It was an old boot, with the words 'Meyers, Toronto' printed inside.

'This is Sir Henry's missing boot!'

'Stapleton must have thrown it away when he came along here.'

30   'Correct. He used it to make the hound attack Sir Henry. We can be sure now that he has gone this way.'

But we did not find Stapleton. There was nothing to show what had happened to him. We could only guess that he had fallen into one of the bog-holes of Grimpen

35   Mire.

13

THE COMPLETE STORY

The younger Rodger Baskerville

It was a cold and foggy night at the end of November. Holmes and I were in our sitting-room in Baker Street. We were discussing the Baskerville case.

'I talked to Mrs Stapleton twice,' said Holmes. 'She told me everything. Stapleton was a member of the Baskerville family. He was a son of Rodger Baskerville, the younger brother of Sir Charles. Rodger went to South America because people in England did not like him. It was believed that he had died in South America without marrying. But this was not true.

'He did marry, and had a son, who was also named Rodger Baskerville. The son married Beryl Garcia, one of the most beautiful women in Costa Rica. The younger Rodger Baskerville cheated people out of a lot of money there, so he came back to England with his wife. He changed his name to Vandeleur, and set up a school.

'The school was successful at first, but later it met with difficulties. It was then closed down. Vandeleur then changed his name to Stapleton, and came to Dartmoor. He had found out that he was heir to the Baskerville fortune, after Sir Charles and Sir Henry.

'He introduced his wife as his sister to people in Dartmoor. He wanted to win the friendship of Sir Charles and the other neighbours. He must have hoped to make Sir Charles fall in love with his wife. But she did not want to do this. Stapleton even beat her, but she would not be persuaded.

'Sir Charles himself had told Stapleton about the legend of the hound. It was clear to Stapleton that

Sir Charles believed in the legend. He knew that the old man had a very weak heart. A shock could easily kill him.

'He bought a very big dog in London. He brought it to Dartmoor by train. Here, Stapleton walked with the animal only when it was dark. He did not want his neighbours to see him with the dog. During his butterfly-hunting, he found a hiding-place in Grimpen Mire. This was where he kept the hound.

'But Stapleton had a problem with his plan. He wanted to give Sir Charles a bad shock, so he often waited with his hound on the moor at night. But Sir Charles never left his house when it was dark.

'Then Stapleton found a way out of this. He was helping the unfortunate woman, Mrs Laura Lyons, and he asked Sir Charles to help her too. Laura Lyons did not know that Stapleton had a wife, and in time, she fell in love with him. He asked her to marry him. Because of this, the woman was willing to believe anything he told her, and do anything he said.

Holmes explains Sir Charles's death

'Dr Mortimer then advised Sir Charles to leave Baskerville Hall. Stapleton knew that he would not be able to do anything if Sir Charles left for London. So he made Mrs Lyons write a letter asking Sir Charles to meet her outside Baskerville Hall on the evening before he left. Then, after the letter had been sent, Stapleton persuaded Mrs Lyons not to go.

'That evening, Stapleton brought the animal close to the gate of the Yew Alley, where the old man would be waiting. When the hound saw Sir Charles, it jumped over the gate and chased him. In the dark, the animal was very frightening to look at. Stapleton had put the chemical, phosphorus, on it, to make it look as if it was on fire. Sir Charles tried to run away, but at the end of the alley he fell dead from a heart attack.

'Only Sir Charles's footprints could be seen on the path because the hound ran on the grass beside it. When the hound found that Sir Charles was dead, it did not attack him. That is why there were no marks on the dead man. But the hound must have come near and smelled him. In doing this, it left the footprints which Dr Mortimer saw. Stapleton then called his hound away and took it back to its hiding-place in Grimpen Mire.

'It was a very clever plan. Nobody would have found out anything. Mrs Stapleton knew about the dog, and about her husband's plan to get the Baskerville fortune. Mrs Lyons knew about the letter to Sir Charles. But Mrs Stapleton was very afraid of her husband, and Mrs Lyons was in love with him. Stapleton thought the two women would never tell anyone what they knew.

'But it was not so easy to murder Sir Henry. Stapleton first thought of killing him in London. But he did not trust his wife because she would not help him. He did not dare leave her by herself at Merripit House. She would lose her fear of him.

'Because of this he brought her to London with him. They stayed at the Mexborough Hotel. Stapleton locked his wife in the hotel room while he followed Dr Mortimer to Baker Street. He had changed his appearance, of course, and later followed the doctor to the Northumberland Hotel.

'Mrs Stapleton wanted to warn Sir Henry, but she was too frightened of her husband to write to him. She knew that if Stapleton should find out, he might kill her. So she cut out words from a newspaper to make a letter.
5   This letter gave Sir Henry his first warning.

How Holmes discovered the truth

'Stapleton had to get something belonging to Sir Henry so that the dog would know Sir Henry's smell. He probably paid some money to the servants in the hotel
10 to help him. But the first boot was new. It had never been worn by Sir Henry, and so it was useless. He returned it and got another — an old one, this time. From this, I knew that the Hound of the Baskervilles could not be a ghost. It was a real animal.
15 'I had already guessed that Sir Henry's enemy was someone from Dartmoor. There was a smell of perfume in the warning letter to Sir Henry. This showed that it had probably been sent by a lady. There are not many ladies who live on Dartmoor and who use perfume. I
20 guessed, then, that the person who sent the letter was Mrs Stapleton, and the person we were looking for was probably Stapleton.

'I decided to watch the man. I could not have done this if I had been with you. Stapleton would have been
25 very careful then. That was the reason I went to the moor secretly.   Young Cartwright came with me. While I watched Stapleton, Cartwright followed you, Watson. In this way, I knew about everything that was happening.

'Your reports were very useful to me, especially the
30 part where you said Stapleton had a school in the north of England. From this, I was able to find out who Stapleton really was. I also learnt from your reports about the escaped prisoner, and the Barrymores.

'By the time you discovered me upon the moor, I already knew everything. But I did not have proof that Stapleton was the murderer. We were sure that the prisoner's death was caused by the hound. We knew that Stapleton actually wanted to kill Sir Henry. But I had no way of proving this.

'So we had to catch him just as he was trying to kill Sir Henry. I had to use Sir Henry to make Stapleton act. My plan was successful but it gave Sir Henry a bad shock.

'I am very sorry about this. I did not know that the hound would be so frightening. But the doctor has said that Sir Henry will soon get well.

'Mrs Stapleton did what her husband told her to because she feared him. Another reason may be that she loved him very much. She agreed to be known as his sister, but she would not take part in murder. She tried to warn Sir Henry several times. At the same time, she wanted to protect her husband.

Stapleton's wife turns against him

'Stapleton himself was a very jealous man. He planned that Sir Henry should fall in love with his wife, but when this happened he became very angry. However, he was able to give some other reason to Sir Henry for his behaviour.

'He asked Sir Henry to go to his house often, because he knew that this would give him the chance he wanted. On the day itself however, his wife suddenly turned against him. She had learned about the escaped prisoner's death. She also knew that the hound was being kept ready in the building in the garden. She asked her husband what he planned to do. They quarrelled angrily. Then Stapleton told her about

Mrs Laura Lyons's love for him. This made his wife very angry. She now hated Stapleton. He knew that she would tell Sir Henry about his evil plan, so he tied her up in a room.'

'He could not have hoped to frighten Sir Henry to death with the hound,' I said. 'Sir Charles was an old man with a weak heart. Sir Henry is a very different type of person.'

'The hound was very fierce and it had not been given food for some time,' replied Holmes. 'It would have attacked Sir Henry.'

'But there is one difficulty,' I said. 'When Sir Henry died, Stapleton would become the heir to the Baskerville property. But how was he going to claim it? He was already known as Stapleton down there. The police would be suspicious.'

'That was a great problem,' answered Holmes. 'Mrs Stapleton told me she had heard her husband talking about it. There were a number of ways in which he could claim the property. One was to go back to South America and do it from there. He did not need to be in England at all. All he had to do was to prove he was Rodger Baskerville to the British Government Office, and once that was done, the rest would not be so difficult.

'Another way would be to say that a friend of his was Rodger Baskerville. He had all the papers and proof to do this.

'Whichever way Stapleton chose, he would have succeeded. We both know that he was very clever.

'And now, my dear Watson, after all these weeks of hard work, we need a rest. I have two tickets for the theatre. Please be ready in half an hour. We can have a little dinner on the way.'

QUESTIONS AND ACTIVITIES

CHAPTER 1

Use these words to fill in the gaps: ***room, dogs, friends, horse, window, hound, farmer, body, moor, home.***

Hugo Baskerville loved the daughter of a (1) _____, but she did not like him. One day Hugo and his (2) _____ carried the girl away from her (3) _____ and locked her in a (4) _____ in Baskerville Hall. She escaped through a (5) _____ and started running across the (6) _____. Hugo was angry and let the hunting (7) _____ out to chase after her. Then he followed them on his (8) _____. Later, Hugo's friends found the girl lying on the ground, dead, and the (9) _____ of Hugo beside her. Standing over Hugo was a terrible (10) _____.

CHAPTER 2

Put the words at the end of each sentence in the right order.

1 Dr Mortimer knew that Sir Charles was frightened by …   [the] [the] [hound] [legend] [of].

2 Sir Charles had seen a strange animal, and he had heard …   [the] [hound] [of] [a] [cries].

3 Dr Mortimer saw Sir Charles watching an animal that was as …   [a] [big] [small] [as] [horse].

4 Other people had seen a large animal on the moor with a …   [it] [around] [ghostly] [all] [light].

5 In the Alley, Dr Mortimer had noticed the footprints …   [of] [dog] [large] [a] [very].

CHAPTER 3

Choose the right word to say what this part of the chapter is about.

Sir Charles must have been waiting for someone he did not want the (1) **servants/neighbours** to see. He was old and in poor health, but he waited (2) **outside/inside** the house when the weather was cold and (3) **dry/wet**. He stood in the Alley by the (4) **door/gate** for at least five (5) **minutes/hours**. The footprints showed that he had (6) **stood/moved** on his (7) **feet/toes**, away from the (8) **house/moor**. He must have been very frightened of something.

CHAPTER 4

Put the letters of these words in the right order. The first one is 'under'.

Dr Mortimer told Holmes that (1) **denur** Sir Charles's will, Barrymore and his (2) **fiwe** received £500 each. Dr Mortimer received £1,000. A (3) **brunem** of other people were given small (4) **unstoam**. Sir Henry received £750,000. Dr Mortimer said that if Sir Henry died, the (5) **troppery** could not go to Sir Charles's (6) **regunoy** brother because he had already died, (7) **irreduman**. Everything would go to a (8) **soinuc** of the Baskervilles, called Mr James Desmond.

CHAPTER 5

*Complete the sentences with these phrases: **a frightening place, his family home, the prison at Princeton, a woman crying.***

1   When Sir Henry saw the moor, he was happy to be returning to _____.
2   Sir Henry and Watson heard that a murderer had escaped from _____.
3   Sir Henry said he would put some lights in front of Baskerville Hall because he thought it was _____.
4   When Watson went to bed, he heard a strange sound inside the house, like _____.

CHAPTER 6

Correct the mistakes in this paragraph: there are nine altogether. The first one is that 'terrible' should be 'wonderful'.

Stapleton thought the moor was a <u>terrible</u> place. Many people knew it better than he did. When they met, Miss Stapleton thought Dr Watson was Sir Charles. She told him to go back to Baskerville Hall immediately. She did not seem to like living in Grimpen, and when she talked she kept listening to her brother. Dr Watson became very friendly with Miss Stapleton, but Stapleton did not seem to want her to marry a poor man.

CHAPTER 7

The sentences marked (b) are in the wrong paragraphs. Which paragraphs should they go in?

1 (a) Watson and Sir Henry decided to watch Barrymore.
   (b) <u>They saw Barrymore going into the same room as before.</u>
   (c) At three o'clock someone walked quietly past the door.
2 (a) Sir Henry and Dr Watson went out into the corridor.
   (b) <u>Barrymore did not want to say anything.</u>
   (c) He stood by the same window, looking out at the moor.
3 (a) Sir Henry asked him what he was doing.
   (b) <u>They stayed awake in Sir Henry's room.</u>
   (c) Then Mrs Barrymore explained that they were giving food to the escaped criminal.

CHAPTER 8

Which of these statements are true? What is wrong with the false statements?

1 Barrymore found the ashes of a burnt letter.
2 The letter had come the day after Sir Charles died.
3 It had come from Coombe Tracey.
4 It was the second letter that had come that day.
5 The note asked Sir Charles to be at the gate at ten.
6 L.L. were the initials of Laura Lyons.

CHAPTER 9

Put the reasons in the right places:

This was true ...	because ...
(1) Laura Lyons needed some money	(a) Sir Charles was planning to go to London the next day.
(2) She wrote a letter to Sir Charles	(b) she was able to get what she needed from another person.
(3) She did not have much time to send the letter	(c) she wanted to divorce her husband.
(4) She could only meet him late in the evening	(d) it was too late to go to Baskerville Hall.
(5) She did not want to meet Sir Charles in his house	(e) it took a long time to get to Baskerville Hall from her home.
(6) After she posted the letter, she did not need Sir Charles's help	(f) it was so late, and he was an unmarried man.
(7) She could not tell Sir Charles about this	(g) she thought he would help her.

CHAPTER 10

Use these words to fill the gaps: **safety, clothes, boot, body, house.**

Selden was killed by the hound because he was wearing Sir Henry's (1) _____. The hound had been given Sir Henry's old (2) _____ to smell, and it thought Selden was Sir Henry. Stapleton thought that the (3) _____ was Sir Henry. He said he had invited Sir Henry to come to his (4) _____. When Sir Henry did not come, Stapleton was worried for his (5) _____.